# WHAT ABOUT DELILAH?

"Uh, this is Elaine Thomas from Hedgerow," the woman on the phone began. She seemed a little upset. "It's about King Perry."

"Isn't that the stallion that Delilah was mated to?" Carole asked.

"Yes," said Mrs. Thomas. "But . . . But—"

"He's okay, isn't he?" Carole asked.

"No," said Mrs. Thomas. "He's dead."

"Dead?" Carole wrote the word on the message pad as she spoke, but it looked odd to her. "Was there an accident or something?"

"No," said Mrs. Thomas. "He was sick. The vet was just here. She says it was swamp fever. Tell Mrs. Reg to call me, will you?"

"Sure," Carole said, hanging up the phone. *Swamp fever*. It didn't sound good. She opened her book to the section on infectious diseases.

There it was—*swamp fever*. Her eyes scanned the page, and then she gasped. *Swamp fever* was the common name of a disease called equine infectious anemia. It was incurable, it was fatal, and, worst of all, it was infectious. If King Perry had it, what about Delilah?

# THE SADDLE CLUB
## SUPER #6

# NIGHTMARE

## BONNIE BRYANT

A SKYLARK BOOK
NEW YORK · TORONTO · LONDON · SYDNEY · AUCKLAND

RL 5, 009–012

NIGHTMARE

A Bantam Skylark Book/October 1997

ISBN 0-553-48428-1

Published simultaneously in the United States and Canada.

Bantam Books are published by Bantam Books, a division of Bantam Doubleday
Dell Publishing Group, Inc. Its trademark, consisting of the words "Bantam
Books" and the portrayal of a rooster, is Registered in U.S. Patent and
Trademark Office and in other countries. Marca Registrada. Bantam Books,
1540 Broadway, New York, New York 10036.

PRINTED IN THE UNITED STATES OF AMERICA
OPM      0 9 8 7 6 5 4

I would like to express my special thanks to Ernie Zirkle, D.V.M. for his patient explanations to me. Everything that's accurate about EIA and epidemiology is because of him. Any mistakes are mine, all mine.

—B.B.

CAROLE HANSON SETTLED into her seat on the bus. She smiled so broadly that it was impossible for the other riders not to notice how happy she was. She didn't notice that they noticed. The only thing she noticed was her happiness.

She was on her way home from an afternoon at Pine Hollow Stables. Pine Hollow was her favorite place in the world, and that alone would normally be enough to make her happy, but today she was especially happy.

Pine Hollow was where she boarded her horse, Starlight. He was a half-Thoroughbred gelding, and as far as she was concerned, he was the most wonderful horse in the world. Considering how wonderful all horses were from Carole's point of view, being considered the most wonderful was quite a compliment. Carole had been taking a private lesson with Max Regnery. Max was her riding instructor, and he was the owner of Pine Hollow. He'd trained many riders and many horses, and he was very particular. In fact, Carole and her two best friends, Stevie Lake and Lisa Atwood, had once counted six mistakes that he corrected for the same rider at the same time! "Heels down, keep your arms steady, straighten that back, show your horse who's in charge, you're on the wrong diagonal, and fasten the strap on your riding hat!" And that was to a rider he thought was doing a pretty good job.

Today, however, he hadn't said that at all to Carole. What he'd said to her was "Nice job, Carole! All your work with Starlight has really paid off. He's behaving like a perfect gentleman and showing you to be the distinguished young rider that you are."

Distinguished. He'd actually said *distinguished*. For a moment, Carole almost wished she kept a diary. This would surely be a red-letter day for that reason alone. However, that wasn't all that had happened.

After her lesson, Carole had joined her friends Stevie and Lisa, who had been watching her. The girls were helping around the stable the way they usually did. That meant that Carole and Stevie and Lisa had been sitting on a bale of hay, talking about what Max had said, until Max's mother, Mrs. Reg, came and told them there were four stalls that still needed mucking out and if they needed a reminder, she could tell them where the pitchforks were kept. They didn't need a reminder.

The girls understood that the only way Pine Hollow could keep its costs down was if everybody pitched in and helped. They were accustomed to making themselves useful.

Carole, Stevie, and Lisa often observed that it would be almost impossible for three girls to be more different from one another and yet completely devoted to one another. Their common bond could be summed up in one word: *horses*. They were all totally horse-crazy. In fact, they were so horse-crazy that they'd formed their own club called The Saddle Club. It was a simple club because it had only two rules. The first was that the members had to be horse-crazy. They all passed that requirement with flying colors. The second was that they had to be willing to help one another out, anytime, anyplace, anyhow. That was a trickier requirement because the girls got into tough scrapes, and it took a lot of imagination, some scheming, some precision, and a fair amount of luck to come to one another's aid successfully. What they'd discovered was that helping could be a lot of fun, too, and that was why these three very different girls were always together.

Of the three horse-crazy girls, Carole was the horse-craziest. She was certain that whatever her future was, it was going to be with horses. Naturally, she'd always own them, or at least one. She'd also ride and would probably compete. She might teach, too. And then, she loved training—and did it well, as Max had reminded her today—so maybe she'd be a trainer. Some days she asked herself if there was anything more exciting than watching a foal be born and then grow into a fine riding horse. Those days, she decided she'd be a breeder. She had spent a lot of time working with Judy Barker, the stable's vet. She'd learned a lot about diagnosing and dosing ailing horses. Could there be anything more wonderful than saving a horse's life? Perhaps she'd be a vet. Carole suspected that one day she'd have to make a decision—or at least cut out a few of the options—but for now, she had a hope that she could actually do all of them.

When it came to horses, Carole never missed the tiniest detail. She wasn't as good as Max at spotting a half dozen mistakes at a time, but she never forgot to give a horse special feed when it was required. She might leave her own jacket at home on a chilly fall day, but she'd never forget to put a cozy blanket on Starlight so that he wouldn't get cold at night. She might leave her school book bag on the table in the morning, but she'd never forget to bring her riding clothes to school.

Carole's house was on the edge of town, which was why she had taken the bus from Pine Hollow. Sometimes she envied her friends their quick walk home from the stable, but living so far away gave her father a shorter commute to the Marine Corps base where he worked. He was a colonel. Carole lived alone with him in the first house they'd ever had that wasn't on a base. Carole's mother had died a few years earlier of cancer. She had loved having a real home of her own, and Carole and her father loved it and took care of it for her now that she was gone. Carole didn't talk about her mother very much, but she thought of her often. She treasured the memories of times spent with her, playing together, cooking together, just being together. Although Carole was quite certain she had the best dad in the whole world, that didn't mean she didn't miss her mother. Even now, riding on the bus, Carole wished she could tell her mother what a great day this had been.

Lisa Atwood was a year older than Carole and Stevie. While Carole could be quite forgetful about a lot of things that didn't have to do with horses, it seemed to everyone that Lisa was just about incapable of ever being forgetful. She was totally organized. She was always perfectly dressed and groomed. She didn't get smudges or rips. She never turned in a homework assignment late, and she almost never got anything less than an A. She was the kind of student who didn't just read the three books the teacher required from the summer reading list, she tried to read all twenty!

In a crisis, Lisa was coolheaded, logical, and straightforward. She was never intimidated by a large project. She'd break it down into small components and attack it with a plan that actually made sense.

Lisa lived with her mother and father in a house right

down the street from Stevie's house. Everything in the house was always as neat and organized as everything else about Lisa.

Lisa was also multitalented. Her mother believed that her daughter should be well-rounded (though Stevie insisted that that meant she was supposed to eat a lot!). Mrs. Atwood had seen to it that Lisa had instruction in a number of areas she considered critical to the well-roundedness of a proper young lady. Lisa had taken lessons in dance (ballet, ballroom, even tap), art (painting and sculpture), sewing, knitting, and walking with a book on her head for posture. In another girl, all these lessons might have combined to make a pretty snobbish teenager; in Lisa's case, they only added to her enormous fund of knowledge about almost everything.

Lisa was the newest rider in The Saddle Club. Both Carole and Stevie had started riding when they were little girls. But Lisa had approached riding the same way she did everything else. She was methodical, thorough, and precise. She studied hard and worked hard, and she learned fast. There were times when Carole and Stevie could give her pointers, but she was almost as good as they were, and she always kept up with them when they went riding together—which was as often as they possibly could.

Both Stevie and Carole owned their own horses. Lisa didn't. She felt that as long as she was still in the process of learning so much, she was better off riding a variety of horses. Stevie and Carole thought that was a good idea, but they also thought it showed some restraint! Most of the time, Lisa rode a Thoroughbred mare named Prancer that had been retired from the racetrack because of a congenital problem with her leg. It was a problem that mattered a lot in a racehorse but not at all in a pleasure and show horse.

Stevie was as different from her two friends as they were from each another. Sometimes her friends thought it was a good thing that The Saddle Club helped each other out, because Stevie was always needing it! There was an irresistible quality to Stevie: a gleam in her eye that spelled fun—and trouble. Stevie was an expert at getting into trouble, and every time her friends pointed that out to her, she reminded them that she was as good at getting out of it as she was at getting into it . . . well, almost. The one part of her school that she seemed to know the very best was the principal's waiting room. She'd spent a lot of time there, but she remarked that some of her finest hours had actually been in the principal's office because she was such an expert at talking the principal out of being angry at her or punishing her. Even her best friends thought the principal might not agree with Stevie about that, though.

Carole glanced out the bus window, barely noticing the lovely countryside they drove through. She thought back to her afternoon at Pine Hollow. It wasn't wonderful just because of what Max had said. It was also wonderful because of what Judy had said.

When Carole had finished riding, she had groomed Starlight and given him water. As she was wiping off Starlight's tack so that it would be clean for the next time she rode, Judy Barker's van arrived at Pine Hollow.

Carole knew what that meant: Judy was bringing Delilah home. Delilah was one of Pine Hollow's loveliest mares. She was lovely in every sense of the word. She was lovely because she was pretty. Although every serious rider knew that a horse's looks were the least important part of the horse, a golden palomino like Delilah was a feast for the eyes. Even lovelier was her personality. Delilah was a gentle mare, always trying to please her rider or handler. Almost everyone who ever rode Delilah became a fan of hers. Carole was no exception.

Delilah was returning to Pine Hollow from a very important visit at another stable near Pine Hollow called Hedgerow Farms. She had been mated with Hedgerow's prize stallion, and everybody was hoping they would soon find out she was carrying a foal. She deserved special treatment.

Carole had helped Judy bring Delilah out of the van and return her to her clean home stall. Carole looked at her very closely, hoping for some indication of impending motherhood, but the horse didn't give a sign.

Clearly, the only thing on Delilah's mind was a nice chomp on some hay and a drink of fresh water. Carole had given her a final pat, closed the stable door, and clicked the lock.

Judy had thanked her for her help. That had reminded Carole of something she had wanted to ask her about.

"Can you take a look at Nero while you're here?" Carole asked.

"Sure, what's up?"

"Well, he seems a little off. I'm not sure I can explain it, but he seems restless. It's probably nothing. He hasn't been ridden in a couple of days and that might be why, but, well, I don't know . . ."

"We'll just see," said Judy. The two of them walked over to Nero's stall. He was a big old black gelding, part quarter horse. He'd been at Pine Hollow for years. He'd been trained by Max's father. He always seemed unflappable, which was why it struck Carole as odd that he was being restless and fussy now.

Judy just watched the horse for a minute. At first Nero just watched her back. Then he stomped his rear right foot on the stable floor, shook his head, swished his tail, and stepped back. He raised his rear right foot again, almost as if trying to scratch his belly, and then reached for his flank with his nose.

"Could that be colic?" Carole asked.

"Bingo," said Judy. "It's subtle, but it's there—classic

9

colic symptoms, the restlessness and trying to get at his belly. He's not really feeling bad yet, but if you hadn't noticed, he'd be feeling awful in a very short while."

Judy then went to her truck, got her medical bag, and returned to give Nero a full checkup. Before long, she had confirmed their suspicions and given the horse the medicine he needed.

"You might have saved his life, you know. Without early treatment, this kind of colic can be deadly. Good work, Carole. I thank you, Max thanks you, but most of all Nero thanks you."

Carole had looked at the horse. He hadn't looked terribly grateful right then. He eyed Carole and Judy suspiciously. Carole didn't mind that he hadn't enjoyed his medical treatment. Horses didn't always know what was good for them. But Carole seemed to. Judy said she'd saved his life.

As Carole stepped off the bus, she was still undecided. Which one of her exciting pieces of news would she share with her father first: being a distinguished rider or a life-saving veterinary assistant?

What a nice decision that was to have to make.

CAROLE SLIPPED HER key into the front door and was pleased to see that it wasn't locked. That meant her father was already home. She pushed the door open, stepped in, and called out, "Dad! I'm home. And guess what?"

Her father stepped out of the kitchen and reached out to give her a welcoming hug.

"I've got some news for you, too," he said. "You go first."

Carole went to drop her riding gear bag in the foyer, but she found that her usual drop point was taken up— by a suitcase.

"No, I think you'd better go first," she said uneasily. She had a feeling she wasn't going to like her father's

11

news much. It would be better to know sooner than to worry about it.

He hugged her reassuringly and they walked into the kitchen and sat at the table. It was their usual place for serious talks. This made Carole even more uneasy.

"Honey, I have to go away for a while," he began.

"I figured that when I saw your suitcase," she said. "Where? And how long?"

"That's the hard part," he said. "I can't say. I mean, I know, more or less, where I'll be and how long I'll be gone, but this is a classified operation and I can't tell anyone."

"Even me?" Carole asked, the news sinking in.

"Even you, my darling. It's the law and I've got to follow it, even when it hurts. I'm going to be okay. Nothing to worry about, I promise. It's you we have to take care of. I thought we might call Aunt Joanna and Uncle Willie to see if you could stay with them—"

"But they live in Florida!" Carole exclaimed.

"Great weather," said her dad.

"But that's so far away. You must think you're going to be gone a really long time . . ." She was near panic.

"No, no, that's not necessarily true," Colonel Hanson said. He reached for her hand and held it tightly. "I didn't mean to scare you. I thought maybe this might be an opportunity for you to have a nice long visit with them. But not too long. Really, not too long. I'm sure."

Carole breathed deeply. She knew that as a Marine,

her father had to go where the Corps sent him, and if it was a classified mission, she couldn't press for information. She also knew that it wouldn't be fair to him to show how worried she was. Then *he'd* just be worried. If he had to be away, doing something important and secret, then he had to be able to do it well. If he spent all his time worrying about Carole, he might mess up, and she hated to think what that might mean. She didn't want to cry. She swallowed hard.

"Um, this isn't a good time to leave school," she said. "It's, like, the middle of the semester. Can't I stay here?"

"Alone?" her father asked.

"No, I mean like with one of my friends. That way I won't miss school, and I won't miss Starlight."

She bit her lip right after she said Starlight's name. Carole had always found comfort in being with horses. When her mother was ill and the world was topsy-turvy, horses and riding had been a safe haven for her. As long as she could ride, something was right in the world. She couldn't lose that now. She just had to stay near Starlight.

It didn't take too long to arrange. Together they decided that it would make the most sense to ask if Carole could stay with Lisa's family. Now that Lisa's brother had graduated from college and was working in New York, Carole might be able to use his bedroom.

Colonel Hanson called the Atwoods and made the arrangements. Carole wanted to talk to Lisa, but she

13

wasn't home yet. Her mother thought she was at the library. That didn't surprise Carole. Lisa spent a lot of time at the library—and she put the time to good use.

Mrs. Atwood told Carole she'd have Lisa call when she got home, and in the meantime, they were happy she'd be visiting them. She was welcoming—warm and kind. Carole knew she was trying to be especially nice, and that made her uncomfortable. That meant that Mrs. Atwood thought it was as awful as Carole did that her father was going away so mysteriously.

She hung up the phone and put on her best smile before she turned to face her dad.

"That settles that," he said. "Now, what's your news?"

Carole had no idea what he was talking about.

LISA FROWNED AT the history paper in her hand. It had her name on it. It said "A" at the top. Normally that would have been enough to satisfy her that she'd done her best. Today, it wasn't enough.

She stared at the pile of books in front of her. She was trying to learn everything there was to know about the buildup of arms in Germany in the 1930s. She thought it might be a good topic for her term paper, which would be due in the spring.

She thought she'd done a good enough job on the paper she'd just gotten back, but when Mr. Mathios had decided to read one student's paper out loud to the class, it wasn't Lisa's paper. It was Fiona Jamieson's.

Lisa stood up and took the pile of books to the re-

15

turn desk. The library was closing. It was time to go home.

Lisa shoved her paper into her book bag. As she walked slowly home, it was as if she could still hear Mr. Mathios reading Fiona's paper. " 'Virtual political vacuum,' " she muttered. That was how Fiona had described war-torn Europe at the end of World War I. Mr. Mathios loved it. Lisa did, too. She just wished she'd written it.

Lisa actually liked Fiona Jamieson. She was a nice girl—very hardworking, and everything she did was good. In fact, everything she did was as good as everything Lisa did. They had almost identical grades all through junior high school. She and Fiona were in eighth grade and would be graduating to high school in the spring. What Lisa wanted, more than anything, was to be valedictorian at her junior-high graduation. The valedictorian was the person with the best academic record in the class, and being valedictorian meant getting special privileges, like course choices, in high school. It also meant it would be on her record when she applied to college. She knew that would look good to any college admissions officer. Yes, this was a time when second place meant losing.

"Wait a minute," Lisa said to herself. "I'm forgetting something. I'm forgetting that trying to be the very best—better than everybody at everything all the time—may seem like a good idea, but it's not always good for me."

16

Lisa's compulsion to be the best sometimes got her in trouble. At summer camp, it had made her lose sight of a lot of things that mattered, like her friends. She'd gotten so tied up in excelling that she'd refused to eat half her meals, worried her friends and her parents half to death, and ended up in a therapist's office.

The therapist was really helpful sometimes. Her name was Susan, and she'd helped Lisa see that she was using her own excellence and her ability to ignore food in order to control her universe. If she couldn't control her success at some things, she could at least control her appetite. Susan had shown Lisa how twisted that thinking could be. Proving that she could be in control of her body wasn't the same as doing what she wanted to do. Now, with Susan's help, Lisa was eating properly again. She was also trying to learn that her best was good enough, even if somebody else happened to be better.

*Whew*, Lisa said to herself, finally realizing what a terrible road she had been heading down. Doing her best was the only thing that mattered. Being better than Fiona wasn't at all important.

She turned the final corner onto her street, shifted her bag to the other shoulder, and headed straight for her door. By the time she got there, all thoughts of beating Fiona had gone from her head. She was totally focused on making herself a schedule for her term paper so that she'd have all the work done on time. Beginning early and sticking to her schedule was a sure road to a great paper.

"Hi, Mom, Dad—I'm home!" Lisa called out.

Lisa's mother was in the kitchen and her father was reading the paper in the living room. They greeted her warmly and she kissed them both. When she came down from putting her book bag in her room, she returned to the kitchen to give her mother a hand with dinner.

Mrs. Atwood gave Lisa the potato peeler, a small pile of potatoes, and a surprising piece of information all at the same time.

"Guess what? We're going to have a houseguest!" Mrs. Atwood said. "Carole is going to come stay with us while her father is away on a business trip. No, I guess it's not really a business trip when you work for the Marine Corps, but anyway, he's got to go someplace and he's not sure how long he'll be gone, but I promised him we'll take good care of Carole while he's away. Isn't that great, dear? Colonel Hanson has to leave at dawn, so Carole will be here before breakfast. You'll be able to walk to school together. It'll be just like having a sister!"

*Carole? Here? Maybe for a long time? What could be better?* Lisa felt her pulse quicken with anticipation. They'd stay up until midnight every night talking about horses and riding and Pine Hollow. If Lisa and Carole were both at the Atwoods', that meant Stevie would be there most of the time, too. It was going to be like the world's longest sleepover.

18

They could do their homework together every night. It wasn't as if they had the same assignments. Lisa was in the class ahead of Carole and Stevie. That had come in handy sometimes when her friends needed help with their homework. Both Carole and Stevie were pretty good at school, but they weren't as good as Lisa, and they often asked her to explain something their teachers hadn't made quite clear. Lisa was good at that, and she never begrudged them her experience. They'd been more than helpful to her when it came to riding.

She had a mental image of Carole sitting in the big comfortable chair in her room, studying pre-algebra while Lisa worked on her paper. It was a cozy image.

"What's $x$ squared times $x$ cubed?" she'd ask.

"$X$ to the fifth," Lisa would say.

"Why?" Carole would ask.

And Lisa would explain it to her, even if it meant losing her train of thought in the book about Germany in the 1930s. That was what it meant to be part of The Saddle Club—helping. She'd be glad to help.

Lisa's mother was speaking, and Lisa realized she hadn't heard anything she'd said.

". . . well, she must find it frightening, you know, since her father can't even tell her how long he'll be gone. I guess that's just part of being in the service. We'll have to be sure to be there for Carole. I'm glad she's staying with us. You two get along so well."

"Definitely, Mom," Lisa said, picking up another potato to peel. Her mother was right. They did get along well. It would be wonderful to have Carole there, even if it wouldn't be wonderful for Carole. Although Carole rarely talked about her mother, Lisa knew she was often on Carole's mind. Lisa thought the only thing worse than losing one parent would be losing two parents. As long as Colonel Hanson was away in an unknown place for an unspecified length of time, it was going to feel as if he were lost. Helping Carole with her pre-algebra might not be anywhere near as difficult as helping her with her worry about her father. And that was what friends were for.

Speaking of friends, Lisa had to call Stevie right away. For one thing, she couldn't wait to tell her that Carole was coming to stay—for a long time. She also wanted to ask Stevie if she could ask her brother Chad about something.

Chad was currently very interested in airplanes. It was just possible he'd have a book with some information about Messerschmitts and the Krupp family in the 1930s. If Carole was going to be staying with Lisa for a while, it was going to take a lot of Lisa's time, and that meant it was all the more important to get to work on her paper right away.

Totally oblivious to the chaos around her, Stevie fluffed her pillow and kept reading her book.

Well, the chaos was really outside her door. All three of her brothers were having a pillow fight in the hallway. They weren't fighting with one another, either. The pillows were all aimed at her door—in retaliation for the fact that Stevie had locked their bikes with a chain that morning and then had forgotten to tell them that she'd changed the combination on the lock. But that was a long time ago. Stevie had practically forgotten about it. How could they still be harping on it?

The fact was that it didn't matter to her anymore. She'd forgiven them for whatever it was they'd done to her that made her lock the bikes up. It was now time for them to forgive her. She kept her attention turned so completely to her book that she never even noticed when the pillow-pummeling of her door stopped.

The book was *The Path to Freedom* by Elizabeth Wallingford Johnson. It was the story of a young slave woman's escape on the Underground Railroad. Hallie, the young woman in the book, had been born a slave on a plantation in Georgia. She had had a baby, and she loved this child, whom she called Esther, more than her own life. When the baby turned five and was old enough to do work, she was sold to another plantation. Hallie made up her mind to find Esther and run away with her to safety and freedom in Canada. When they'd left the last station at dusk, the farmer had told her to look for the rock with the cave and the arrow-shaped cleft in it. "It points the way," he said.

*Hallie crouched down behind a boulder. She could feel Esther's sweet breath on her neck as the child slept, oblivious to the danger that lurked behind every tree in the woods. Hallie almost regretted her decision to travel on this, the night of the full moon, but time was a luxury she and Esther didn't have. She'd heard the slave hunter's hounds baying all day long. Now what darkness there was would have to hide them through the long night. The moon cast eerie shadows through the bare branches of the forest overhead.*

22

Stevie shivered. She could almost feel the warm breath of the child on her own neck.

*Hallie felt the rough surface of the boulder that made a shelter with a second rock, which seemed to be a flat piece that had broken off the larger boulder. It was like a cave, perched, as it was, on the hillside. On the larger boulder, she could feel something, like a mark cut into the stone. Was that the arrow? Had she found her marker? She would not know until dawn—if dawn ever came for her.*

*Nearby, she could hear the gentle bubbling of a brook. Fresh, cool water awaited them. She peered through the darkness. Yes, there was the creek. There was another boulder next to it, silhouetted in the moonlight.*

*Swiftly and silently, Hallie stood and ran to the creek. It would refresh them. It would also help hide their scent from the hounds. She knelt and put her fingers into the water, then scooped a handful of its cool goodness into her mouth.*

*Without a word, she woke her sleeping child and gave her a drink, too. Then she returned to the slight shelter of the rock. They could rest awhile. She slid into the crevice, bringing Esther with her. She pulled some dry leaves after them, hoping to cover her tracks and hoping to hide their presence.*

*There was a noise. Hallie held her breath. Esther's eyes opened wide in terror. Hallie put a warning finger to her lips. Esther was silent.*

*Boots. Someone was walking nearby in boots. They shuffled the leaves carelessly, pausing, then moved forward, to the creek and back to the rock. Then they stopped close enough to Hallie's face for her to smell the grease that had been used to polish them.*

*"Nobody here," said the man wearing the boots.*

*"But I could swear—" another voice protested.*

*"Nobody here," the first voice said insistently.*

*Hallie couldn't help herself. She looked up. The man was looking right at her. "Let's go," he told his companion.*

Stevie let out her breath when she was sure the man in the leather boots and his companion were out of the area. "Whew!" she said out loud. She could hardly remember when a book had seemed so real to her.

She felt as if she'd been right there with Hallie and Esther, and she loved it. It was as if she could see the moonlight filtering through the bare branches of the woods, as if she knew those woods, then or now. It could have been Willow Creek.

With a start, Stevie realized that it *could* have been. Really. The book was based on the diaries of a real runaway slave. The author's note at the beginning explained that Hallie's actual route had never been known. It was a historical puzzle that might never be solved.

Stevie reread the passage that described the land. The hill, the direction of the moonlight, the rock with the crevice where Hallie and Esther hid. And then there was the creek and the rocks next to it.

It wasn't just that Stevie felt as if she'd been there. She was sure she'd been there—not a hundred and fifty years ago, but recently. It was a perfect description of the woods behind Pine Hollow! If this was a historical puzzle, then Stevie was a historical detective, and she was well on her way to cracking her first case!

Eagerly she picked up the book. She couldn't wait to read the rest of it so that she'd know for sure.

The door of Stevie's room flew open. It was Chad. He dropped a book on her bed, said, "Phone for you. It's Lisa," and left with as much grace as he'd entered with.

Stevie had been so excited about Hallie's route that she hadn't even heard the phone ring. She picked it up now.

"Hi, Lisa," she said. Then she looked at the book Chad had brought her. It was all about World War II aircraft. Wasn't that just like her dorky older brother to give her a big old boring book?

"Did Chad give you the book?" Lisa asked eagerly. "Can you bring it to Pine Hollow tomorrow? Oh, it's going to be great for this paper I'm working on." Lisa chattered on about her latest history project. Since

25

Stevie now had a history project that excited her, she could understand Lisa's enthusiasm.

"Oh, and there's other news, too," Lisa said. "Carole's dad has to go on some kind of top secret mission. It's awful because he can't tell anyone where he's going or how long he'll be gone, but the good news is that Carole will stay with me. Won't it be great having her here in our very own neighborhood?"

"Nonstop Saddle Club meetings!" Stevie said excitedly.

"Well, that, of course, and then there will be times when I'll be too busy to spend as much time as I'd like with her, but you'll be practically next door and you can visit with her, too, right?"

"Count on me," said Stevie. Stevie knew that if she'd had those two pieces of news to share with a friend, the fact that Carole was coming for a visit would have come before the history paper. But that was Stevie. This was Lisa. For Lisa, friends were really important, but so were history papers. Thinking about history papers again reminded Stevie she wanted to tell Lisa about *The Path to Freedom*.

"Oh, listen, I'm reading this great historical novel," Stevie said. "I bet you'd love it."

"Is it about Germany in the 1930s?" Lisa asked.

"No way," said Stevie. "It's about—"

"No, the next thing I want to read is that book Chad gave you."

26

"Well, this is a good book and I know Carole will like it. It's about the Underground Railroad. She had a relative who escaped slavery that way, remember?"

Lisa did remember. The man's name was Jackson Foley. Carole had told her the whole fascinating story. Lisa thought it might be interesting sometime to learn more about that part of American history, but not until after she'd finished her current school project.

"It must have been awful for the slaves who fled to freedom," said Lisa.

"Definitely," said Stevie. "From what I've read here, it was worse than that. It was a nightmare."

# 5

"You know, I bet I'll be able to send you a fax through my office machine," said Colonel Hanson.

Carole was next to him in the front seat of their station wagon. He was trying to make her feel better, and she was trying to pretend she felt better so that he wouldn't worry that she was worried. Meanwhile, she didn't want to worry that he was worried while he was gone. It was pretty confusing, and none of it made Carole feel any better.

"That's great, Dad," she said.

"And Sergeant Fowler will always be able to reach me in an emergency. All you have to do is to call her at my office and I'll get the message."

"That's great, Dad," said Carole. She wondered if Sergeant Fowler would consider a serious case of home-sickness—well, really dad-sickness—an emergency. Actually, Sergeant Fowler probably would. She was a wonderful warm woman who tried unsuccessfully to hide those qualities behind her stiff khaki uniform. When it came to Carole's father, and Carole, for that matter, Sergeant Fowler was attentive and kind, so much so that it sometimes seemed as if Colonel Hanson left his daughter at home to go be with his mother at the office.

"I'll call her every once in a while to let her know I'll be late at the stable, just so she won't miss you too much," Carole teased.

Colonel Hanson laughed, and that made both of them feel better.

He pulled to a stop in front of the Atwoods' house. They sat for just a moment.

"I'm going to miss you, baby," he said, giving Carole a hug.

"Me too," said Carole, glad of her father's shoulder to hide her tears.

"And before you know it, I'll be home," he said.

"That's great, Dad," said Carole.

It only took a minute to get Carole's suitcase from the back of the car to the door. Lisa and her mother were waiting in the dim hallway, still wearing bathrobes.

The next few minutes were a jumble of hugs and reas-surances. Carole was welcomed, the Atwoods were thanked by Colonel Hanson, Carole was hugged and reassured by her dad. So were Lisa and Mrs. Atwood. And then he was gone.

Carole stood at the door and watched her father drive down the street in the morning twilight. Lisa stood next to her, her arm across Carole's shoulder. Carole didn't cry until she was sure her father was gone. Lisa gave her another hug, and Mrs. Atwood handed her a tissue. Carole thanked them both and then picked up her suitcase. She needed to be alone for a few minutes, and unpacking was the perfect excuse.

Carole used her unpacking time to try to pull herself together. Her father had been away before. He'd been on lots of trips for the Corps. Sometimes she'd stayed with family or friends. Sometimes she had been able to go along with him. But this wasn't just a trip. This was different, and that was what upset Carole. She didn't know *anything* about the trip, and not knowing was the hardest of all. But it was her father's job. He thought it was an important job, and it was important to do it right. Carole sighed. Most of the time, she was glad her father was in the Marines. Today, however, she had the feeling it would have been nice if he'd had a job that didn't move, like pumping gas at the station in the middle of town. Or maybe he could commute into nearby Washington the way Mr. Atwood and Mr. and Mrs. Lake did. Whenever they took business trips, everybody knew where they were and exactly when they'd get back.

But Carole's father wasn't those people. He was Colonel Hanson, her own beloved, wonderful, funny, gentle, and kind dad. Carole swallowed hard. She'd try to be strong for him.

She closed her now empty suitcase, stored it in the closet, and turned out the closet light just as Lisa nudged open the door.

"All done?" she asked.

"Yep," Carole said. "I'm ready for the day." She hoped she sounded as if she meant it. It was one thing to have her father worry about her. She didn't want her friends and their families worrying as well.

Breakfast at Carole's house was usually a rushed affair. A bowl of cereal, a cup of instant coffee for her father, some orange juice, and then a dash for the bus. At the Atwoods', it was more like a meal. Everybody sat around the table at the same time, eating platefuls of hot food. Here it was a Tuesday, just any old Tuesday, and Mrs. Atwood had made pancakes. Maybe it was just because it was Carole's first breakfast with them. She hoped so, anyway. Otherwise, her father might not recognize her when he got back!

Lisa spooned some hot peaches onto her pancakes. "Carole, wait till you see what it is I'm working on. I got a great idea for my next history paper, and I talked to Chad last night and he's got a book for me. It's about Messerschmitts—you know, the German planes they

31

used in World War Two? Also— Oh, Dad, do you know anything about the German arms buildup between World War One and World War Two?"

"Sure," said Mr. Atwood. "There's a really good book called *The Arms of Krupp* that might be helpful. It's about a family of arms manufacturers in Germany who provided munitions to the Prussians and Germans throughout the nineteenth and twentieth centuries. It might be in your school library, but it will certainly be in the town library."

Carole winced. She wasn't entirely comfortable with talk about arms buildups, even if it was history. Her father was on a top secret mission he couldn't talk about. That could be an arms buildup, too.

Mrs. Atwood seemed to sense Carole's discomfort. She clicked on the television so that they could watch one of the morning shows. At this time of year, they would probably be given an explanation of how to make kids' Halloween costumes safe. That was much nicer to think about than war and conflict. But instead of some woman explaining how to put reflecting tape on a ghost costume, they found themselves watching the morning news.

Carole realized that maybe she would get some hint of where her father might be if there was trouble brewing somewhere. It was a relief to find that the world was relatively peaceful. In fact, there was even talk of a peace summit in Paris. If someone was building up arms somewhere, the morning news didn't know about it.

"Time to go!" Mrs. Atwood announced, clicking off the television set and picking up the empty plates in front of the breakfasters. "I'll see you girls about six o'clock tonight after your ride. Dinner at seven-thirty."

That was the first really nice thought Carole had had that bleak morning. She would go riding that afternoon. As long as she and Starlight could be together, something would be right in her universe.

Carole and Lisa walked briskly toward school. Lisa's house was down the block from Stevie's. Stevie and her brothers didn't go to Willow Creek's public schools. They all went to Fenton Hall, a private school in town that was just far enough away that they had to take a bus. All four of the Lake children were waiting for the bus out in front of their house.

Stevie waved happily to Carole and Lisa, then ran up and gave Carole a hug.

"I'm sorry about your father being away and all, but it sure is great to have you in our very neighborhood. How about a Saddle Club meeting when we get out on the trail at Pine Hollow? There's something I want to show you in the woods."

"It's a date," Carole told her, returning the hug. "See you there about three-thirty, okay?"

"Have you got the book?" Lisa asked Stevie. For a

moment Stevie looked blank; then she realized what Lisa was talking about.

"Oh, sure. You want it now? I'd be glad to give it to you. It weighs a ton!" She reached into her book bag and pulled out Chad's book on airplanes.

"Thanks," Lisa said to Stevie, and then again to Chad. She put the large volume into her own book bag.

"That's great," she said to Carole as they continued along toward school. "This way I can get some reading done during lunch."

As they walked, Carole was once again bemused by her friends. They were so different from one another. It was a good thing they all loved horses or they might not have anything in common!

CAROLE PUT DOWN her grooming tools and buried her face in Starlight's neck. The silky softness of the gelding's coat and mane were familiar and comforting. For the first time in that very long day, Carole felt some respite from her worries and her distress over her dad's sudden departure.

"Oh, Starlight," she said. The horse tilted his chin down so that it pressed gently on her shoulder. It was his way of hugging her back, and it helped a lot.

Starlight always seemed to understand. He'd listened patiently while she told him all about her father's trip and how she was staying with Lisa, and he was listening again as she explained her frustration with her dear friend and hostess.

". . . and if I hear one more word about Messerschmitts or the German arms buildup, I think I'm going to scream! I mean, working hard on a paper is one thing—and a good thing—but this paper isn't due until April and this is October. We're talking six months! That's not hard work, that's obsession, and it's nuts! For one thing, it's going to drive me crazy. For another, really much more serious thing, it may drive Lisa crazy. It's like she's forgotten what can happen to her when she—"

"Am I interrupting something?" Stevie asked, knocking politely on Starlight's stall door.

Carole pulled herself away from her horse and turned, smiling at her friend. "Just a conversation with the one friend I have who never disagrees with me!" she joked.

Stevie laughed. "Speaking of friends, I've just tried to have a conversation with Lisa and the only thing she wanted to talk about was how interesting Chad's book was. I looked at that book last night, and it's not that I'm the best book judge in the world, but it didn't even qualify as moderately interesting as far as I'm concerned. What's with her today?"

"Oh, boy," said Carole. "That's exactly what I was talking to Starlight about when you came in. It's like she's gone off the deep end. You know how she can be."

"I do," said Stevie. "I also know that sometimes these obsessions pass quickly. Not that she won't do a fine job

36

on her paper when she goes to write it, but hopefully she'll realize that it won't take six months of hard labor and she'll ease up. That would be great. I only hope it happens soon."

"Immediately is soon enough for me," Carole said. She handed Stevie a towel for Starlight's final rubdown, and the two of them worked on Starlight together. There was always work to do around horses, and it was always more fun if you did it with a friend. In a minute they'd be grooming Stevie's horse, Belle, together.

"Maybe we just have to wait for a while and see what happens," Stevie suggested.

"I guess," Carole agreed. "And in the meantime, I'll be at her house and can keep an eye on her."

"That's another reason I'm glad you're there," Stevie said. She gave Starlight's coat a final wipe with the cloth and tossed the towel into Carole's grooming bucket. It was Belle's turn now. "Horse number two, coming up!" she declared.

Fifteen minutes later, all three girls were mounted on their horses, ready to have a nice long trail ride together. Troubles and worries melted away for each of them with the rhythm of their horses' easy walks.

Taking a trail ride meant doing whatever they wanted to do, but sometimes that also meant working on skills that they each needed to hone.

"Can you help me with something?" Lisa asked. "I've

been trying to get Prancer to curve her whole body when she makes a turn."

Out in the field, she demonstrated what she was doing and what Prancer was doing. The idea was to have the horse's body follow a smooth, rounded line at a corner. Otherwise turns could be choppy and awkward. In formal English riding, smoothness was highly desirable and choppiness was definitely not.

Carole and Stevie studied Prancer's turns. Stevie spoke first.

"I think it's that you're forgetting to give signals with anything more than your hands. If you only use the reins to turn, then the horse's head leads the way and the rest of her body simply follows. If you use your legs, too, putting a little bit of pressure on the girth with your inside leg and a little bit of pressure behind the girth with your outside leg, Prancer's body will make its own turn. Does that make sense?"

"It does to me. Let me see if it makes any sense to Prancer," Lisa said. She tried another turn. It was like night and day. Instead of a choppy, side-shifting, right-angle turn, she and the mare were making a smooth, gentle, rounded turn.

"Nice work," said Carole.

"I wish it were all so simple," Lisa remarked.

"Well, you're a fast learner," Stevie said, just a bit proud of her own teaching skills.

"Thanks," Lisa said.

The girls proceeded on their ride.

"Did I tell you about Nero?" Carole asked.

"No, what?" Lisa asked. "I just gave him a pat as I walked Prancer out of the stable. He seemed fine. He even nipped at me!"

"I'm glad to hear that. Yesterday he seemed a little off somehow, so when Judy brought Delilah back from Hedgerow, I had her take a look. She said he was in the very early stages of colicking and I might have saved his life!"

"Congratulations!" Stevie said. "See, you really were meant to be a vet."

"Or maybe a breeder," Carole said. "Because, I've got to tell you, I'm getting all excited about the possibility of Delilah having another foal. After all, her last foal is just about perfect!"

The friends all agreed with that. They'd been there to help Delilah when Samson was born, and they'd loved the coal-black foal from the first time they'd seen him. They felt as if they were his aunts, and they'd even helped with a lot of his training.

"Maybe we'll have another little champion," said Stevie.

"Any foal that Delilah has is a champion in my book," said Carole. "Even if he never wins a ribbon."

"What if it's a filly?" asked Lisa.

"Then I hope she's got as sweet a disposition as her mother— What are you doing, Stevie?" Carole said.

This was the third time Stevie had left the trail and ridden Belle around a rock.

"I'm looking for a sign," she said, as if that explained anything.

"A sign?" Lisa asked. "What are you talking about?"

"It's in the book," Stevie explained. Lisa and Carole exchanged glances. Stevie had a way of giving nonanswers to questions and expecting other people to understand everything she wasn't saying.

"Uh, Stevie? What book? What sign?"

"Oh, right," Stevie said. "I started to tell Lisa about it last night, but we got sidetracked with her history project. Well, this is my history project. And I'm sure I'm right."

"And?" Carole asked, somewhat bemused.

"I'm not going to tell you about it. I think I'll keep it a secret for now. But I *will* tell you one—no, make that two—things: It's very close to home, and it happened a long time ago. Now that's a history project, isn't it?"

"I guess it is," Lisa said, but she seemed uncertain. To her a history project was something you looked up in the library. But it was Stevie's project. She could work on it in whatever way she wanted.

"Maybe you'll think this is another crazy idea of

40

mine," said Stevie. "But I'll find it. If it's here, I'll find it."

"Sure," Carole agreed. "It can't be the craziest idea you've ever had. Actually, I'm not sure exactly which idea of yours was the craziest. What do you think, Lisa?" she asked.

"Hmmm," Lisa said thoughtfully. "How about the time she ran for class president at the fund-raising fair while we were entertaining the Italian boys?"

"Pretty good, but not on a par with the, quote, buried treasure, unquote, in England," Carole said.

It was a great game to play. Carole and Lisa took turns recalling Stevie's wildest schemes. It helped them each to remember times that weren't troubled by Colonel Hanson's absence, and there were so many schemes to choose from that there was plenty of fodder for the players. They swapped memories all the way to the creek and back to Pine Hollow. It helped make the trail ride just exactly what all three of them needed.

After a while, Stevie loosened her reins so that she could put both hands on her hips. "You guys!" she said disgustedly. "Those were nothing!"

"Compared to . . . ?" Lisa asked.

"My personal favorite," said Stevie.

"And which was that?"

"The elephant."

Carole hit her forehead with the palm of her hand.

"How could we forget the elephant?" she asked.

The three of them dissolved into giggles.

As they returned to Pine Hollow, they all felt as if the ride had gone too fast and was over too soon. Carole glanced at her watch and could hardly believe that it was almost five o'clock.

Approaching Pine Hollow, the girls paused to watch Max while he gave a lesson to one of his adult students, Betty Johnson, in the schooling ring.

"Look," Stevie said to Lisa. "When Mrs. Johnson makes the same kinds of turns you were making, she doesn't usually bother to move her legs at all. But if— Oh, see what's happening now."

While the girls watched, Max stopped Mrs. Johnson and spoke with her. In a second she got back to work, nudging her horse into a walk. As she approached the next corner, her outside leg moved back ever so slightly. The horse made a smooth turn.

The girls smiled and then waved at Max and Mrs. Johnson as they rode past the schooling ring.

"Good ride?" Mrs. Johnson asked.

"The greatest," Stevie answered.

She knew that Mrs. Johnson always enjoyed a trail ride, too. Now, the next time she went out, her turns would be as good as Lisa's.

CAROLE WIPED THE final speck of dust off Starlight's saddle and yawned. She looked at her watch. It was nearly five-thirty. They'd come in from their ride a half hour earlier, and although they'd meant to have a Saddle Club meeting after the ride, the girls had dispersed quickly.

Stevie had given a hasty explanation about how she was responsible for making dinner that night because of a tiny little food fight she'd instigated with her brothers at breakfast. Carole was glad she wasn't staying at the Lakes'. Stevie's idea of a great snack included things like pistachio ice cream with licorice chips. Carole hated to think what Stevie would come up with for a whole meal.

Lisa, on the other hand, wanted to rush home so that she could watch a program she'd seen advertised on the

History Channel. Carole strongly suspected that the program had to do with Germany in the 1930s, and that was the kind of subject that made her uneasy today. Carole told her friends that she didn't have any reason to rush anywhere. She just wanted to spend some more time at Pine Hollow, where everything was as it should be. She'd take her time cooling Starlight down, then check in on Nero, and then see how Delilah was doing. Carole told Lisa she'd be home soon.

Carole had another nice visit with Starlight, giving him a complete grooming this time. His short summer coat was beginning to grow into a longer winter coat, and it took some attention. While she brushed him, he turned and sniffed at her neck, then nickered in her ear. It made her laugh. That felt very good and confirmed her suspicions that for her, horses were always the surest way to happiness.

"You know," she told Starlight, "when I groom you, I'm doing it because you need it and it's my job, but it's also a way to say thank you for all the wonderful times I've had with you and with other horses as well. No, don't get jealous, you know I love you best of all, but before you came into my life, there were other horses. If there hadn't been, how could I possibly have had anything to judge you by? How would I know you were the best? Anyway, horses have always been good to me, so it's the least I can do to repay you and your, um"—she

44

searched for a word—"colleagues." She laughed at her own statement, but she knew, as she was laughing, that she meant every word of it. Horses had been more to her than she could expect anybody, even Starlight, to understand. She owed Starlight and every other horse more than she could ever repay. That was one of the reasons she was always willing to take on another chore for a horse.

She ended the grooming when Starlight's coat was shiny clean. She fetched his evening ration of hay and a fresh bucket of water.

"See you tomorrow," she said, giving him a final pat on his sweet, soft nose.

Next stop was Nero. He seemed to be a completely different horse from the edgy, uncomfortable gelding she'd seen the night before. The medicine Judy had given him had worked like magic. His eyes were bright. His ears perked up when she approached. She peered over the edge of his stall to check for manure. There was plenty of it, a good sign that the colic was completely cleared up. As if to prove that he was his own usual feisty self, Nero nipped at her hair.

"Enough, boy," Carole said, pulling her head out of his naughty reach. "You're supposed to be thanking me, not biting me."

Nero seemed unrepentant, but Carole still gave him a pat on his neck and then along his face. She'd much rather have him nip at her hair than be sick! She told him to get a good night's sleep and she'd see him the next day.

Delilah's stall was around the corner from Nero's. Delilah liked peace and quiet, so they'd always kept her away from the rush and bustle of the main aisle. Carole smiled to herself, thinking about all the little quirks horses had that people had to be aware of. People needed to make allowances for horses' personalities. Carole was only too happy to do that.

"How're you doing, girl?" Carole asked.

Delilah looked at her serenely. Carole gave the golden-colored mare a gentle pat and then ran her fingers through her silvery mane. Delilah didn't move. She usually preened a bit when she sensed that someone was admiring her beauty. This time she seemed to remain aloof.

Carole felt a tingle of excitement. Could it be? Was Delilah really pregnant? Would she be delivering a new foal next fall? If she was, Carole was the only one who knew yet. It would be her secret for a couple of weeks until the human world knew for sure. For now, the secret was all Delilah's, but Carole thought she was trying to share it with her; Delilah seemed somehow changed.

"Don't worry, girl. I won't tell anyone yet. For now it will be our secret, and I promise I'll take good care of you. Remember how Lisa and Stevie and I took care of you last time?"

Delilah watched and listened. Carole was sure she understood. At the very least, Carole knew that the mare understood her tone of voice, that she was being affectionate and reassuring.

"Well, I know you did most of the work, but we did help, and look what a beautiful young colt you brought into the world—Samson! Your next foal will be just as wonderful, and we'll be just as caring. You don't have a thing to worry about. The Saddle Club will take care of you, now and forever!"

Carole gave the mare a hug. The horse seemed to welcome her affection and didn't pull away as she sometimes did when someone tried to hold her. Carole loved the feel and smell of the big palomino. Her coat was almost as smooth as Starlight's. Delilah felt warm, too. *It must be the glow of excitement about her secret*, thought Carole.

"Oh, I almost forgot something," Carole said, fishing in her jacket pocket. "If you're going to have a foal, or even if you're not, we've got to look after your diet and health very carefully. You'll need plenty of vitamins. We want the strongest, healthiest foal in the whole county. So we'll start you off with a nice dose of beta-carotene, vitamin A, calcium, and phosphate, if I remember my last nutrition lesson properly." Carole pulled out a handful of carrot sticks and offered them to Delilah. The horse looked curious, sniffed, and then stepped back.

That was unlike her. In fact, that was unlike almost any horse. Horses generally loved carrots.

"Are you sure?" Carole asked, holding the carrots out again. Delilah didn't show any more interest the second time than she had the first. It was odd, but it was also quite possible that someone else at the stable had just fed her a snack. A lot of people had missed Delilah while she was at Hedgerow. She was one of Pine Hollow's favorite horses, and now, possibly carrying a foal, she was a prized tenant. She'd probably been stuffed with carrots all day long!

"Oh, I know what it is!" Carole said. "I've heard about how women who are pregnant develop weird food cravings. Next thing you know, you'll be demanding pickles and ice cream! Well, all I can say is, if that's what you want, you can go to the ice cream shop with Stevie. She eats the most amazing things—though I don't ever recall her actually putting pickles on ice cream. Probably just because she never thought of it, and I don't think I'll suggest it, because I couldn't watch her eating it—and she would.

"Okay, so if what you want is weird stuff, I'll try to get it for you, but, believe me, it'll have carrots tucked somewhere in it, because those are really good for you!"

Delilah took in a deep breath and sighed. Carole interpreted that as a sign that she'd understood every word and was now awaiting some pretty exotic food. It made Carole laugh. She gave Delilah a final pat and left her for the evening. Delilah would need good, nutritious food, but she'd also need plenty of rest so that she could deliver a strong, healthy foal early next fall.

All the same, it was a little odd that Delilah didn't want any carrots. Carole thought it might be a good idea to check with someone to be sure she was right about dozens of people already giving Delilah carrots that day.

Max would know. Carole made sure that Delilah's stall was properly locked and then went looking for him. It wasn't hard to find him. It was just almost impossible to talk to him. He was still working with Betty Johnson, who was making a lot of progress in this lesson. When Max was giving a lesson, a herd of wild buffalo could stampede by, and if it didn't happen in the ring where he was working with his student, he'd never notice. Carole waved to Mrs. Johnson, who waved back (no student ever concentrated as well as Max), and then Carole went in search of someone else for information.

Her next choice was Red O'Malley. Red was Pine Hollow's stable hand, generally responsible for seeing to the care and feeding of the horses. He'd want to know if somebody had been giving too many snacks to any horse, especially a horse that might be in a delicate condition.

Red was also easy to find. He was being mobbed by three very young, very eager new riders.

"Let me go first!"

49

"I want to ride the brown pony! Please, please, puh-leeeeeze!"

"You didn't want to ride the brown pony until I said *I* wanted to ride the brown pony!"

Red was holding three saddles and three bridles and was surrounded by utter confusion. He could have used some help, for sure, but Carole knew that if he spotted her, she'd be hooked into helping the little girls, and sorting out which one got to ride "the brown pony" was low on her priority list at the moment. She felt like a skunk, but it was getting late and she'd be due back at the Atwoods' for dinner long before this tiny threesome was ready to call it quits.

Carole ducked behind one of the many poles in the stable and slunk away in search of Mrs. Reg.

"We are very proud of how well we look after our boarders, Mr. Terban. If you decide to board Columbia here, I'm sure you'll be pleased with her care."

That meant Mrs. Reg was giving the grand tour of the stable to a prospective customer. Since Pine Hollow relied on the income from boarding horses, this was important. Carole *could* interrupt, especially if she was showing the kind of concern Pine Hollow gave to all its horses, but she'd have to pick her moment carefully.

Mr. Terban was not going to be easy to convince. "Mrs. Regnery," he said, "I'd like to see where the horses are turned out. The other stable I visited had a large area

50

where the horses were allowed to run free for at least half an hour every day if they weren't being ridden."

"We don't have one exercise area as you describe, Mr. Terban. We have a series of them, plus the larger fields beyond our own rings and paddocks. Come this way and I'll show you."

This was definitely not the right time to interrupt. Mrs. Reg led the potential client toward the schooling ring and explained one of Pine Hollow's traditions as they went.

"We call this the good-luck horseshoe," she said. "Every rider who leaves the stable is asked to touch this before beginning his or her ride. And that will include you, too, if you decide to ride here. Among the things we're proud of is our safety record. No rider here has ever been seriously hurt."

Carole smiled. She was as willing as anybody to believe in the magic of a U-shaped chunk of iron, but she also knew that touching the horseshoe on the way out was a simple reminder to every rider that horses were big animals and safety was important—for both the horse and the rider. She watched as Mr. Terban reached up and touched the horseshoe. He smiled at Mrs. Reg.

Carole nodded. That was it. He'd bring Columbia here—partly because of the horseshoe, partly because the exercise area was so much larger than the other stable he'd visited, and mostly because Pine Hollow was a wonderful stable and only a fool wouldn't recognize that.

Well, that was good news for Pine Hollow, but it left Carole without anybody to ask about Delilah and carrots. She wasn't really in a hurry (except for not wanting to get embroiled in the "brown pony" melee with Red). She could sit in Mrs. Reg's office for a few minutes and see if either Max or Mrs. Reg came by and had a few minutes for her.

Carole went into the office and picked a book from the reading shelf. It was *A Horse Around the House* by Patricia Jacobson and Marcia Hayes, and it was the most useful general reference book about horses and horse care that Carole knew. She flipped it open randomly and began reading. It didn't matter what section she'd opened to; she'd learn something useful. This time she found herself learning something she hadn't known about braiding.

She was reminding herself how to sew mane braids to keep them tidy when the phone rang, startling her. It didn't surprise her that she'd gotten so deeply into what she was reading that she'd lost all track of where she was, to the point that the phone made her jump. After all, she'd been reading about horses!

She ignored the phone for two rings. Pine Hollow had strict rules about who was supposed to answer the phone. Number one was Mrs. Reg. It was her phone and her job to answer it. But it wasn't ringing in the field or the paddock where Carole knew Mrs. Reg was with Mr. Terban.

52

Number two was Max. Max was in the schooling ring with Mrs. Johnson. He would have no idea that the phone was ringing at all, nor would he consider leaving a student, even a good one like Mrs. Johnson, for a minute to do something as mundane as answer the telephone.

That left Red—now probably totally tangled in the reins of three sets of tack, trying to get the ponies ready before three little girls killed one another.

And then there was Carole. She was in the office, she wasn't busy, and she knew she could be responsible. She picked up the phone on its fourth ring.

"Pine Hollow Stables, this is Carole Hanson speaking," she said, trying to sound adult and professional.

"Uh, this is Elaine Thomas from Hedgerow," the woman began. She seemed a little upset.

"Oh, I was just visiting Delilah," Carole said, glad of the opportunity to thank Mrs. Thomas for taking good care of the horse during her stay. "She seems just great. She got back here safe and sound. I can't wait until we learn if she's carrying a foal. I'm just sure—"

"No, hold on. That's not what I'm calling about."

"I'm sorry," Carole said. She picked up a pencil and a clean pad of paper so that she could take a message. She promised herself to write neatly. She wanted to be sure the message was complete and legible.

"It's about King Perry," said Mrs. Thomas. Carole wrote *King Perry* on the pad.

"Isn't that the stallion that Delilah was mated to?" she asked.

"Yes," said Mrs. Thomas. "But . . . But—"

"He's okay, isn't he?" Carole asked.

"No," said Mrs. Thomas. "He's dead."

"Dead?" Carole wrote the word on the pad as she spoke, but it looked odd to her. How could the stallion that had so recently been mated with Delilah be dead? "Was there an accident or something?" she asked, though she thought it was a dumb question. Of course there had been. How awful it must have been!

"No," said Mrs. Thomas. "He was sick. The vet was just here. She says it was swamp fever. Tell Mrs. Reg to call me, will you?"

"Sure," Carole said. The phone went dead in her hand. She hung up, made a note on the pad that Mrs. Reg should call Mrs. Thomas, and then scratched her head as she often did when she was trying to remember something.

*Swamp fever.* It didn't sound good, but there were so many fevers and infections horses could get that she couldn't always remember which was which. She turned to the book she'd been reading, checked the index, and opened to the section on infectious diseases.

There it was—*swamp fever*. Her eyes scanned the page, and then she gasped. *Swamp fever* was the common name of a disease called equine infectious anemia, or EIA. It was incurable, it was fatal, and, worst of all,

54

it was infectious. If King Perry had it, what about Delilah?

Carole picked up the phone to call Judy Barker and tell her to get there right away. It wasn't necessary, though. Before she could even dial the number, a familiar truck pulled into the Pine Hollow driveway. Judy knew this was an emergency. She had come already.

8

IT SEEMED AS IF everything happened at once then. Judy arrived, Max finished his lesson with Mrs. Johnson, Mrs. Reg returned to her office with Mr. Terban, and Red sent a gleeful trio of little girls back to their parents, all promising they would never fight over a pony again.

The look on Judy's face told Max, Mrs. Reg, and Red that this was not a casual visit. Carole handed Mrs. Reg the phone message from Mrs. Thomas.

"Oh, no," she said. "King Perry just died of swamp fever." While Max and Red took in the horrible news, Mrs. Reg turned to her newest customer. "Mr. Terban, I'm afraid I've wasted your time. We can't take any new boarders now. We're about to be quarantined."

"Oh?" he said, perturbed. "Then I guess I should go back to Hedgerow Farms."

"No, you're going to have to go elsewhere," Judy said. "They'll be quarantined, too. Okay, let's get to work," she said to the others, dismissing Mr. Terban. Carole suspected that Mr. Terban would think they were being rude, but that wasn't the case at all. It was simply that there wasn't a minute to waste!

"My first job is to check on Delilah," said Judy. "Carole, come with me. You can help with the checkup. Max, Red, here are some vials and needles. We need to draw a blood sample from every horse in the stable. Please label them carefully. Now, first of all, is there a place where we can isolate Delilah?"

"How about the extra stall in the feed shed?" Carole suggested. Max nodded in agreement.

"Let's go," said Judy. She left Mrs. Reg's office so quickly that Carole found herself running to catch up. Without pause, Judy opened Delilah's stall, clipped on a lead rope, and cast a practiced eye over the mare.

"No obvious symptoms," Judy said. Carole found herself sighing with relief, though she recognized that it might not mean anything. Obvious symptoms would indicate an advanced stage of the disease. It couldn't move that quickly, could it?

Carole took the lead rope from Judy and tugged gently to make Delilah follow her to the feed shed. Words kept tumbling through her mind. *Incurable, infectious,* and *fa-*

*tal.* She knew what they all meant. What she didn't know was how they applied in the case of this disease. Was it certain that Delilah had it? How would they know?

"This is a serious disease, Carole," Judy said, as if she could read Carole's mind. "It's serious and it's deadly—as we already know from King Perry's death."

"How do they get it?" Carole asked.

"Only by blood transfer," said Judy. "There are two ways we know it goes from horse to horse. One is from the careless use of a needle. If a vet or caretaker uses a needle on one horse that has the disease and then doesn't clean the needle properly before using it on the next patient, the disease can be carried that way. More likely and more common—since any sensible caretaker cleans needles thoroughly—is that the disease is carried by insects. Commonly it's the tabanid in the deerfly family. The insect will bite one victim that already has the disease, and then one that doesn't. If the virus is in the blood of the first horse, it won't be cleaned from the biting part of the insect before it gets to the second horse, and that's how the second one becomes infected."

"Is it really common?" Carole asked.

"No, not really," said Judy. "And the reason it isn't is because we are so extremely careful about it. Any horse that moves from one stable to another is tested. Any horse that crosses a state line is tested. For example, Pine Hollow horses are tested yearly—more often if they're going to shows. As soon as there is any sign of the disease, the stable is quarantined. That means no horses can come or go or be anywhere with any other horse from other stables until the quarantine is lifted."

"How long does that take? Until we get the results of the blood tests?" asked Carole.

"No, we'll have the results of the first set of tests in a couple of days. But since the incubation period of the disease can be as long as forty-five days, Pine Hollow will be quarantined for the full forty-five days."

Carole was horrified. Was she going to be separated from Starlight? "You mean nobody can be here for a month and a half?"

"No, that's not what it means. You can come here and you can ride. You can take lessons, go on short trail rides, whatever you want, as long as you stay on Pine Hollow property. What you can't do is take the horses off the property or have any other horses visit. The only protection quarantine gives is for horses outside the infected area. It's intended to contain the disease within a single horse population—in this case all the horses and ponies at Pine Hollow and Hedgerow Farms. And the quarantine is really very conservative. Most horses that have been infected will test positive and begin to show symptoms within about two weeks."

Carole looked back at Delilah. She looked fine. She still seemed a bit aloof, and she was definitely curious about why she was being taken to the feed shed, but she seemed healthy enough. She even paused to take a nibble of fresh grass.

"These flies, are they everywhere?" Carole asked.

"They're not uncommon," said Judy. "They tend to live in swampy areas, which is why stables in swampy areas and near wetlands are particularly susceptible. They are a summer insect, and this warm fall must have kept them around."

"Pine Hollow isn't near any swamps," Carole said.

"Right, but Hedgerow Farms is," Judy said. "It could also be that King Perry was infected during the summer and nobody knew or suspected it until he began to show symptoms. In rare cases, a horse can be infected long before any symptoms show up. In some cases, symptoms never show up. There are horses who are just carriers of the disease, like Typhoid Mary."

"Who?" Carole asked.

"She was a woman who never got sick but managed to infect a lot of other people with a terrible disease. There was an epidemic all around her, and finally all the victims were traced to this one common source. They tested her and found she was a carrier but had no active symptoms."

Carole led Delilah into the feed shed. It had been the original stable at Pine Hollow when Max's grandfather had bought the place. There was room for three horses in it. Two of the stalls were filled with bags of grains, and the loft had a supply of hay and wood shavings. Because the feed was kept there, it was especially important to keep the place free of insects and rodents. That made it a particularly good place for Delilah to wait out her quarantine. She'd be isolated. Unlike those on the stable, the doors on the feed shed were screened and generally shut. She'd be protected, and so would the other horses.

Carole cross-tied Delilah in the shed's small open area so that Judy could give her a physical exam and draw the blood sample. While Judy began checking the mare, Carole put fresh wood shavings in the single open stall. She wanted Delilah's temporary home to be extra nice. Delilah might enjoy peace and quiet, but it could be hard on her to be so isolated from her stablemates for forty-five days.

As she worked, Carole found her mind wandering to the larger possible consequences of King Perry's death. She'd read about this disease. It was bad. Judy wasn't telling the worst of it. Swamp fever had been known to sweep through entire stables. The thought took Carole's breath away.

Judy removed her stethoscope from Delilah's belly and spoke to Carole. "Now, don't go and think about all the awful things that could happen." Judy was clearly reading Carole's mind—though Carole suspected the tears that had brimmed in her eyes when she considered what might happen to Starlight had given her away.

"The point is that Delilah has been back here less

than twenty-four hours. We don't have a large tabanid population, particularly at this time of year. Delilah's at risk, certainly. But most of the other horses really aren't. We have to treat them as if they are at risk because it would be idiotic not to—and illegal as well—but I think their prospects are good. For now, Delilah isn't showing any symptoms, so the blood test is really important. We have to be patient and responsible."

Carole finished freshening the stall, added some hay to the feeder, and poured fresh water into a hanging bucket. Then she held Delilah's halter and patted the mare while Judy completed her physical examination and drew the blood sample.

"She looks okay to me," said Judy. "No symptoms at all. We'll just have to send the blood to the lab and wait."

"And cross our fingers?" Carole suggested.

"That too," said Judy.

Carole unhitched the cross-ties and closed Delilah securely into her new temporary home. They both patted the mare and said good night before turning off the light and leaving, closing the door securely behind them.

"Not one fly is going to get in there!" Carole said.

"Good idea," said Judy.

As they walked back to the main stable, Judy told Carole more about the disease and its consequences. None of the news sounded very good to Carole.

"First of all, it's only transmitted by blood, nothing

else," said Judy, "so the fact that she was mated to King Perry wouldn't mean anything whatsoever, unless there were flies around. Next, it's a disease that horses get, that's why it's called *equine* infectious anemia. People don't get it at all. There is no danger whatsoever to humans—"

"Except maybe breaking their hearts," Carole said.

"Yes, there's that," Judy agreed.

9

LISA HEARD CAROLE'S footsteps coming up the walk to the house and opened the door to welcome her home. It had been a long day, Carole's first without her father there. It would be good for her to have a smiling face at the door.

But a smiling face wasn't what Lisa got in return. "Carole! Are you okay?" she asked. "Is something wrong—your dad?" She barely whispered the last words.

"Is something wrong with Dad, too?" Carole asked, looking even more alarmed, if that was possible.

"No, no, nothing at all. But what do you mean, 'too'? What *is* wrong?"

Carole walked through the door, greeting Lisa's parents absently as she walked past the den to the stairs.

64

"It's at Pine Hollow," Carole said. "I wish I'd never answered the phone."

"What are you talking about?" Lisa asked.

Carole went into her temporary bedroom, dropped her book bag and her riding clothes bag on the bed, then flopped down on it herself.

"Oh, Lisa," she began, and then she told her friend about everything that had happened—from the phone call until she'd left Pine Hollow.

"So now Judy has all the blood samples and she's taken them to the lab," Carole concluded. "She says it'll be two to four days until we know anything. Of course, since Delilah got back so recently, she couldn't have infected any of the other horses at Pine Hollow yet—or, I mean, she could have infected them, but if she did, it wouldn't show up in their blood tests yet. But what if it wasn't just King Perry who has it and there's a lot of it around and, and . . . ?" She couldn't even go on.

Lisa felt every bit as bad as Carole did, but she wasn't also feeling the stress of her father's departure, a super-early morning, and a frantic afternoon. She was simply calmer than Carole was.

"Take it easy, Carole," she said, sitting down on the bed next to Carole. Idly she began rubbing her friend's back to comfort her. "This disease isn't all that common, although it is deadly and has to be taken seriously."

"Easy? How can I? Do you know what they do to

horses that test positive for it? I mean horses that have the disease or carry it—like Typhoid Mary?"

"Sure, they isolate them," Lisa said.

"For *life*," Carole said. "They have to spend the rest of their lives away from every other horse, whether they are showing symptoms or not, covered by nets so they can't spread it. That is if they're lucky. Most of the time, if they test positive for it, a kind owner or a compassionate vet will have the horse put down, euthanized, *killed*." She spat out the last word, and it was followed by a gush of tears. "And what if Delilah has it? That tiny foal will never be born!" she said through her sobs.

It would be awful if Delilah was sick with swamp fever and died as King Perry had. But if she'd infected other horses at Pine Hollow . . . ? That could mean the end of Pine Hollow as they knew it. No, it couldn't be. She couldn't even think about it.

"Carole," Lisa said, trying to sound calm even though she was worried, too. "It just doesn't make sense that any of the other horses would be infected now. You said that it's really late in the season for tabanid flies, and Delilah's only just returned. It's going to be okay."

Carole took the tissue Lisa handed her. She tried to stop crying and calm herself down. Lisa was a friend, a good one, a logical, cool-thinking one. She was right. It wasn't sensible to assume that all the horses at Pine Hollow were going to be infected. It didn't even make a lot of sense to assume that Delilah was going to be infected.

66

Judy had looked her over. She hadn't seen anything. Delilah was fine.

And then Carole remembered the carrots. Delilah didn't want carrots. Delilah always wanted carrots. She'd never refused them, even when she'd just eaten her breakfast. *Carrots*. No, Carole couldn't think about that now.

Mrs. Atwood called up the stairs then. "Carole, dear, it's that nice Sergeant Fowler on the phone for you."

They hadn't even heard the phone ring.

Her father. How could she be worried about horses when she should be worried about her father? What did Sergeant Fowler know? How could there be news already? Was it bad?

"Carole, pick up the phone and ask her, will you?" Lisa prodded her. Carole hadn't even realized she'd been talking out loud.

"Hi?" she said tentatively into the phone.

"Oh, Carole, it's Sergeant Fowler calling. I just wanted to let you know that I had a fax from your father already. He's doing just fine and asked me to let you know that." Carole sighed with relief. At least something was going right today. "They've arrived safely and have been deployed to their quarters," Sergeant Fowler continued. Carole could almost see it. In her mind, he was in a bleak, pale, isolated desert. Thousands and thousands of soldiers were there, hunkering down in tents for the night. Outside, a sandstorm, camels fenced into hastily assembled paddocks. Inside, her father, his computer with built-in fax machine, and nothing on his mind except for her. She smiled to herself. She loved him so much. And he felt the same way about her. He was the best dad in the world.

"And he wanted me to let you know that he really likes the place where he is," Sergeant Fowler said. "In fact, he said that one day he hopes to take you there. That's all for now, dear. I'll let you know when I hear from him again."

Carole hung up the phone and shared the message with Lisa.

"See, I told you he'd be fine," she said.

"I guess," Carole said. Then she wondered why her father wanted to take her to the desert. All that sand? *It must be sort of starkly beautiful*, she thought. *And then the oases are supposed to be great, interesting food, exotic markets, camels, and, of course, horses.* Arabians were bred for their stamina in the desert. Yes, that must be what her father knew she'd like about it—lots and lots of horses.

Mrs. Atwood's voice came up the stairs again.

"Dinner's ready, girls!"

"Oh no," Carole said. "I didn't do anything useful and I haven't even showered!"

"No problem," said Lisa. "For one thing, I helped with dinner and set the table, so you're off the hook on that. For another, it's corned beef and cabbage, and that stuff has such a strong smell that Mom and Dad will never notice a little eau de horse on you. And for a third, we can do the dishes together, and just because you missed table-setting, I'll make you dry and put away."

Carole laughed. "Deal," she said. "Only I still think I'll wash up a tiny bit before I join the family. Can you delay a little?"

"No problem. I'll go pour milk veeeeeeeery sloooooowly. You've got three minutes—okay?"

"Okay."

Five minutes later, Carole joined the Atwoods at the dinner table, apologizing for keeping them waiting.

"It's no problem, Carole," Mrs. Atwood assured her. "I somewhat misjudged the doneness of the potatoes, so your timing actually turned out to be just about perfect."

Mr. Atwood handed Carole a plate. "Lisa told us about the message from your dad. It sounds like everything is going fine there."

"Yes, it does," Carole agreed.

"But what's this Lisa was telling me about the horses?" he asked.

"What's wrong with the horses?" Mrs. Atwood asked.

"It's a disease," Carole began explaining.

"They're sick?"

"Um, no—I mean, I don't think so. What I really mean is that I hope not. Nobody's sick except King Perry, but he isn't sick anymore. Oh, I'd better begin at the beginning."

Carole started to explain the whole thing, but it wasn't easy because Mrs. Atwood kept interrupting. She was a kind woman and a loving mother, but she wasn't a very good listener and had a nasty habit of jumping to conclusions.

"I'll call Dr. Peterson right away," she said, getting up from the table.

"What?" Lisa asked.

"Well, you girls will have to be tested, too. This is a deadly disease."

"It's a horse disease, Mom," Lisa said. "People don't get it."

"But if people get bitten by the flies . . . and you children are so susceptible to all kinds of infections—"

"Its full name is equine infectious anemia," Lisa explained slowly. "*Equine* means it's a horse disease. People don't get it."

"I'll call Dr. Peterson anyway," said Mrs. Atwood.

"Why don't you call Judy Barker first?" Carole suggested. "Perhaps she can explain it better than Lisa and I seem to be doing."

"All right, I'll do that," said Mrs. Atwood, continuing to the phone.

"I think we can wait until after dinner," said Mr. Atwood. "From what Carole says, Dr. Barker has had a very long day and could use a quiet time for her dinner before you call her."

"Okay, dear," said Mrs. Atwood.

Briefly, it crossed Carole's mind that it must be difficult for Lisa to spend so much time with a mother who constantly needed to be calmed and reassured. Maybe that was one of the things that made Lisa so good at reassuring. Carole could still feel the nice little glow of comfort from the back rub Lisa had given her while she cried. Carole was very glad that Lisa was her friend.

The two things that Carole and Lisa both noticed about dinner that night was that they'd spent the meal taking turns explaining everything they knew about EIA and that neither of them had eaten very much. In the face of such a dire problem, food didn't seem important.

Then, when dinner was over, the two girls walked to Stevie's house to tell her what had happened. Stevie was a much better listener than Mrs. Atwood.

"Oh, poor Belle!" Stevie said when Carole told her that she'd helped get blood samples from all the horses. Belle was a good-natured horse most of the time, but she wasn't a very good patient.

"She didn't fuss at all," Carole told Stevie. "I held her halter and told her knock-knock jokes. I was trying to make her think I was you."

Lisa and Stevie laughed. Everybody knew that it was good to talk calmly to a horse when it was upset, and Stevie had decided that if she liked knock-knock jokes, her horse undoubtedly did, too.

"Which ones?" Stevie asked.

"Isabel necessary on a bicycle," Carole said.

"Well, she's already heard that one," Stevie said. "If she believed you were me, she probably thought I'd slipped a cog!"

"I didn't say I fooled her," Carole said. "I just said I tried."

"Thanks," Stevie said.

The girls knew that their joking contrasted sharply with the concern each of them felt, but it was a way of keeping themselves from crying, which seemed to be the only alternative. Given a choice, laughter was almost always better.

"I bet those horses are going to be fine," Lisa said. "I mean, the more I think about it, the surer I am that they just weren't exposed—well, probably not, anyway. I mean, Delilah was at Hedgerow Farms for three weeks and she's not showing any symptoms. That's what Judy said, right?"

"Right," Carole said, but she didn't sound as if she meant it, and her friends picked up on that immediately. Stevie glanced over at Lisa, who shrugged quickly, out of Carole's sight. Carole could agree out loud; she could hope that Judy was right; but her jacket pocket still had carrots in it that belonged to Delilah. She couldn't bring herself to tell anybody that, because then she might have to acknowledge out loud that something was wrong, really wrong. Loss of appetite was only one symptom of swamp fever, but it was a symptom.

Carole and Lisa didn't stay long at Stevie's house. For

one thing, Stevie still had to clean up the kitchen. For another, so did Lisa and Carole. And then Lisa mentioned that she wanted to leave plenty of time later in the evening to read the book Chad had given her.

They wouldn't all be able to meet at Pine Hollow the next day because Lisa said she had to go to the library. Stevie frowned ever so slightly when she heard that, but she remembered that she and Carole weren't going to try to stop Lisa from doing her work. They were just going to watch to see if they ought to. Okay, so she'd wait. Stevie said she'd see Carole at Pine Hollow the next afternoon.

"I know, I know," said Carole. "You just want to make sure that Belle is okay after having to hear that old knock-knock joke from me, right?"

There was a twinkle in Stevie's eyes. "Well, I did hear a good one today," she said. "I'd tell it to you now, but I want to try it out on Belle first."

Lisa slammed her lunch tray down next to Carole.

"Not a happy camper today?" Carole asked, surmising that so far, at least, Lisa wasn't having a good day.

"Definitely not," Lisa said. She examined the contents of her tray to see if she'd done any damage. Since only a container of yogurt and an apple rested on it, no harm was done.

"What's the matter?" Carole asked, somewhat more sympathetically.

"It's that Fiona," Lisa said. "You wouldn't believe her! Kissing up to the teacher all through history class. Mr. Mathios couldn't even see through it. He just seemed to lap it up. Every time she said anything, he said, 'Very good, Fiona,' like nothing anybody else in the class had to say was very good."

Carole opened her milk carton and considered the situation. "Well, what did he say when you commented on something?" she asked.

"Once he said, 'Good question,' and another time he said he was glad I'd mentioned something. Oh, and about my quiz he said, 'Nice work, Lisa,' like that was a compliment or something."

"Sounds like he said pretty much the same thing to you that he did to Fiona," Carole said, treading carefully.

"No, it's not the same at all," Lisa countered. "Maybe you just had to be there, but I'm telling you, this girl is the teacher's pet, and it's making me sick to my stomach. She is *so* obvious!"

It was all Carole could do to keep from asking Lisa if she thought other people might consider Lisa the teacher's pet in some of her classes. Lisa was such a good student that teachers naturally liked and respected her. If that wasn't being a teacher's pet, Carole wasn't sure what was. This was a sensitive area for Lisa, though, especially where it concerned Fiona.

"Lisa, do you think it's possible that you might be envious of Fiona?" Carole asked.

"Envious?" Lisa asked in return, saying the word as if it was totally odious to her. "How could I be envious of her?"

"Well, it seems like you wish Mr. Mathios had given

you the attention he gave to Fiona. Would it feel nicer if he'd said, 'Very good, Lisa,' instead of 'Fiona'?"

"No, you don't get this at all," Lisa said, disturbed that her friend was so completely missing the point. The point was that Fiona was trying so hard to be nice to Mr. Mathios, and he didn't even see through it!

"I think I do get it," Carole said. "Really, I do, Lisa. It's frustrating and annoying when someone else is getting the attention and admiration that you've earned and deserve. But the fact is that not everybody can always be 'best,' whether that means in one class on one day or even in a class throughout a year. You are a very good student, you get nothing but As—"

"I got a B-plus in math last year."

"That was only the spring semester grade. Your overall grade for the year was a nice little A, as usual. You don't always have to get As," Carole said. "It's okay if you are better at some things than others *and* it's okay if somebody else is better than you are at something."

"No, you don't understand, Carole," Lisa said. "The point is that you and Stevie can be satisfied with second best—"

Carole could feel anger rising in her. She didn't like being told she was second rate. But she knew that this conversation wasn't really about her. It was about Lisa, who seemed to need a reminder of what was important and what wasn't. Carole stayed as calm as she could

76

manage and spoke to her friend as warmly as possible under the circumstances.

"That's not fair," Carole said. "And besides, second best doesn't matter at all as long as you, or I, or anyone, knows that they've done their personal best. If I work at something really hard, put everything I can into it, and it's not wonderful, I have the satisfaction of knowing that I did the best I could. Maybe I learned something from doing it and maybe the next time I do it, I'll do it better. You should keep that in mind."

"But you're always the best at riding," Lisa said. "It's your way of knowing that you are the best at something."

"Maybe," Carole said. "But I'm not always the best. A lot of times other people do things better than I do. Stevie's much better at dressage than I am."

"Stevie's horse is better at dressage than Starlight," Lisa said.

"No, not really. Stevie just enjoys dressage more than I do, so she works at it harder and Belle has learned better."

"But you're both better riders than I am."

"I'm not sure that's true," said Carole. "But I am sure that if it is true, it doesn't matter. You are my friend and Stevie's friend and that's much more important to us than if you can do a turn on the forehand or a flying change."

Lisa looked distressed. She took two spoonfuls of her yogurt and then pushed the tray away. She'd spent more than an hour the previous Saturday trying to get Prancer to do a flying change, and she hadn't managed it. That was another area in which she was failing, just like in history.

Carole wasn't done. She had one more thing to say to her friend. "There's something else I'm sure of," she said. "I do understand how much success in school means to you, but it's not really the way I feel about horses. No matter how much I love horses—working with them, riding, taking care of them—I'm never going to let them make me sick."

Lisa opened her mouth to say something, but before she could speak, the bell rang. Lunch was over. It was time to get back to class.

"I'm going to the library after school," Lisa said, standing up, "so I'll see you at home. And, uh, thanks."

Carole watched Lisa head for her math class and knew that Lisa's "Thanks" was sincere. Her message had been received, though not welcomed. It was okay. Sometimes being a friend meant hurting someone's feelings. Carole knew that being honest and being right weren't always fun.

She picked her books up from the table and then gave it a final glance. Lisa's lunch was almost completely uneaten. She'd just tasted the yogurt and left the apple untouched. Carole was going to Pine Hollow after

78

school. She could put the apple to good use. She stuck it in her book bag, knowing instinctively that, unlike either Stevie or Lisa, she wouldn't forget she'd brought the apple for the horses at Pine Hollow. Lisa was right about one thing. When it came to horses, Carole always did her very best.

CAROLE DROPPED HER book bag in her cubby at Pine Hollow, but not before she had fished Lisa's apple out of it. She found a knife by the refrigerator and cut the apple into quarters.

It hadn't been a very good afternoon for Carole. She'd spent most of it wondering where her father was and what he was doing. She'd spent the rest of it worrying that Lisa would be angry with her for speaking her mind. She'd spent almost none of it paying attention to anything any of her teachers had said. Nobody, but nobody, was saying, "Very good, Carole," that afternoon.

Finally, after her last class had ended, she'd grabbed her things and run for the door. Going to Pine Hollow was always "very good, Carole," as far as she was concerned. And then, on her way out, she'd seen Lisa, who was heading for the library. Lisa had waved cheerfully and told her she'd see her later. Carole hoped that meant that she had taken in Carole's message and wasn't angry. It could also mean that Carole's message hadn't begun to sink in, and therefore Lisa wasn't holding a grudge because she didn't know she had anything to

79

hold a grudge against. Life could be so complicated sometimes!

Carole put the apple pieces in a plastic bag and headed straight for the feed shed. Delilah seemed to be waiting patiently for her. She looked up solemnly when Carole walked in. Carole checked her over. The mare looked okay. Nothing was obviously wrong, though she was a little more restrained than usual. But then, usually, she was surrounded by a lot of activity, and that could stimulate any horse to be livelier.

"How you doing, girl?" Carole asked. Delilah nudged her gently, then nuzzled her neck. Carole loved that feeling. She took one of the apple pieces from the plastic bag and held it out to Delilah.

"It's a present from Lisa," Carole explained to the mare. Delilah sniffed at it curiously and then picked it up with her teeth, brushing the palm of Carole's hands with her soft warm lips. She muched methodically, dripping some saliva and apple bits, swallowed, and then waited expectantly for a follow-up to the snack.

"Oh, no you don't," Carole told her. "You're not the only horse I care about in this place. You have to share this apple with Starlight, Belle, and, um, well, I guess Nero, to celebrate his getting well. I just wanted to be sure you were okay. I'll come back again tomorrow to see you. Okay?"

Delilah didn't answer. Carole took that for an okay.

She gave the horse a final hug and headed out of the feed shed to dole out the rest of the apple.

The first person she saw when she got back to the stable was Stevie, who was busily picking out Belle's hooves and chattering to the mare as she worked.

Carole picked up a mane comb from Stevie's grooming bucket and went to work next to Stevie.

"Trying out that new knock-knock joke?" she asked.

"I did," Stevie said. "She didn't like it, though. She said she'd already heard it from Barq."

"Figures," Carole said, smiling to herself. Stevie was truly irrepressible, and it was one of her most endearing qualities.

"So, how was today?" Stevie asked. "Any more word from your dad?"

"Not yet," Carole said. "Though I haven't been back to the Atwoods', so who knows? But I had lunch with Lisa, and I've got to tell you, she's getting more and more obsessive about her history class and her history paper. She was envious of this girl, Fiona Jamieson, because the teacher had said, 'Very good, Fiona,' to her in class but he'd only said, 'Good question' to Lisa."

"Oh, boy," said Stevie. "I think if a teacher told me I'd asked a good question, I'd leap up and down for joy. Oh, no, that's not right. One of my teachers did say that to me one time because I'd asked if the wailing sound outside the room was the fire alarm going off."

81

"Stevie, it's a good story, but I don't think it's going to do Lisa much good. I think we've got to stop keeping an eye on her and start a Saddle Club project that'll save her from going overboard with this competitive student thing."

"I know, I know. You're right," Stevie said. "But what on earth can we do to help her?"

"That's it!" said Carole.

"What's it?" Stevie asked.

"We have to help her. If we do some of the work on her paper, it'll take some pressure off her," Carole said.

"We can't do that. It's called plagiarism or something like that. It has to be her own work, and besides, there isn't a history teacher in the world who wouldn't be able to tell the difference between a paper I wrote and one Lisa wrote."

"No, I don't mean that we write it for her. Of course we can't do that. But we can do some of the background work, you know, like Chad did just by giving her a book she can use. Maybe if we point out to her where she can find some good information, that would be helpful. Since your family has had a computer longer than anyone else's, you're the best typist in The Saddle Club. You could do some of the typing for her. See what I mean?" Carole asked.

"I guess I do," Stevie said. "But you know, sometimes it scares me when I look at my friends and begin to see myself. You guys are getting more and more like me every day."

"Does that mean I'm going to have to put licorice chips on peppermint ice cream?" Carole asked in mock horror.

"Hmmm. Sounds delicious," Stevie said. "But I don't think we have time for a trip to TD's tonight." TD's was the ice cream parlor where The Saddle Club often treated themselves while they had club meetings. "No, we've got to finish up here and then get to my house for a trip on the Internet."

They redoubled their efforts to make Belle's coat gleam, because after that was done, they had to groom Starlight and visit Nero and give out the rest of the apple. There was a lot of horsework to be done before they could attempt progress on Lisa's homework.

## 11

"Uh-oh," STEVIE SAID, looking at the computer screen in front of her.

"What's the matter?" Carole asked, looking up from the newspaper that had held her interest while Stevie clicked away at the keyboard. "Didn't you get anything with the search?"

They were using the Lakes' on-line service to try to find material for Lisa's paper. It had taken a long time to get the information they wanted. It wasn't that the computer was slow; it was that there were so many other things to do on their way to the arms buildup in Germany. They'd spent some time reading on-line bulletin boards, sending messages, playing games, and chatting with friends before they'd actually gotten started on their search.

"No, that's not the problem. I got too much," Stevie said. Carole put down the newspaper. It was too full of talk about the summit meeting in Paris to have anything about desert operations. She looked over Stevie's shoulder at the computer screen. The screen informed them that they had found more than twenty thousand matches to their key word.

"Perhaps we should narrow the search just a little bit," Carole suggested.

"How utterly logical of you," Stevie teased. "First you've got a wild scheme in your head, and then you've got a sensible suggestion. It's hard to tell if you're getting more like me or more like Lisa every day!"

"Peer pressure," Carole said. "It's supposed to make you crazy. It's clearly working—or else it's just you guys who are making me crazy!"

Stevie typed in several words this time, not just *Germany*, and set the search mechanism to work.

When the results came up, there were only twenty-five items. That was much more manageable than twenty thousand. She printed the list, then set about searching for something else.

"What are you looking for now?" Carole asked, peering at the screen. "Underground Railroad? Are you trying to get a head start on Lisa's paper for American history next year?"

Stevie laughed. "No, not really. I'm just interested in the subject. I'm reading a book about it—it's really good, and I'll lend it to you when I'm done. I thought I might be able to get some background information—Hmmm." She studied the screen as her results came up. She pressed Print and then logged off. "I'll look at that later," she said.

"Is this a novel you're reading or a history book?" Carole asked.

"It's a novel," said Stevie. "But it's based on the diary of a real person. It's a great book, but it's especially interesting . . ." Stevie hesitated. Was she being silly in thinking that Hallie and Esther must have come near where they lived now? She didn't think she was, but she thought her friends might describe the idea as "one of Stevie's wild schemes." She wasn't in the mood for ridicule at the moment, so she decided to keep her peace. ". . . especially interesting because it's based on something that definitely did happen. Anyway, you're going to like the book a lot. It's called *The Path to Freedom*, by Elizabeth Wallingford Johnson." What she didn't say was that she was convinced Carole and Lisa would both love it because Stevie was planning to prove that a lot of the book happened practically in their backyards. Or, more exactly, in Pine Hollow's backyard.

"Sounds familiar," Carole said. "I must have heard about it or read something somewhere."

"Well, people must talk about it because it's really good," said Stevie.

"Maybe," said Carole. "But whatever, it's definitely familiar."

"Stevie! Dinner!" her brother Chad called loudly from the dining room.

Carole and Stevie had been so busy playing on the computer that they hadn't noticed how much time had flown by.

"Oh no!" said Carole. "I'm late!"

"Well, it's a good thing you're only going a couple of houses away, then."

Carole answered her, but she knew that Stevie never heard her because she was running so fast out the door.

How could she do this? She was a guest at the Atwoods'. She knew what time they ate dinner. She'd almost kept them waiting last night, and tonight it was even worse.

She flew down the street, ran up the walkway, and burst through the door.

"I'm sorry, I'm sorry," she cried out as she entered the Atwoods' home. "I didn't mean to be late. I just got caught up in something at Stevie's house."

She ran upstairs and put her things in her borrowed room. She washed her hands quickly and then went downstairs as fast as she could. Lisa and her parents had started eating already. Mr. Atwood paused to serve up a plate for Carole.

"I really am sorry," she said, slipping into her chair.

"That's all right, Carole. We understand," said Mrs. Atwood. "But we do eat at seven-thirty, so perhaps it would be a good idea for you to make a note of that in the future. You shouldn't have to rush so before dinner. It's not good for the digestion, you know."

Carole gulped. On the one hand, Mrs. Atwood sounded very kind, as if she wasn't at all annoyed and really did understand that Carole hadn't meant to be late. On the other hand, Carole *was* late. She'd kept them waiting, and they'd finally gone ahead and eaten without her. Anxiety swept through her. She wanted to be a good guest. She wanted to be welcome. She *was* a good guest, she *was* welcome, but she'd made a mistake and it seemed very difficult to gauge exactly how serious it was. Everybody smiled. At least Mr. and Mrs. Atwood smiled a little. Lisa smiled a lot and continued talking to her parents about the work she'd done on her paper that afternoon. What did the little smiles from Lisa's parents mean? Would it have been easier on her if they'd been obviously annoyed? When her own father was annoyed with her, Carole always knew it. It was easy to tell with him because he said it right out. With the Atwoods, it wasn't so simple. The result was that even if they weren't annoyed with her, she felt as if they were, and that made her more uncomfortable than she would have been if they clearly had been annoyed. Life was complicated when your father was thousands of miles

88

away, gone for an unspecified time to an unknown place!

Carole took the dinner plate, thanking Mr. Atwood as she did so, and set it down in front of her. It was a piece of baked chicken, some rice and peas. It was a very normal dinner, the kind of thing she and her father often ate, but it was still different. It wasn't that it was bad. Mrs. Atwood was a good cook and Carole had always enjoyed everything she'd eaten at Lisa's house. It was more that it was different. "Different" wasn't what Carole wished she had right then. What she wanted instead was exactly what she almost always had at dinnertime: her father. She wanted to taste his crispy baked chicken, cooked with what he called his special secret seasonings. (Near as Carole could tell, that meant salt and pepper.)

Just thinking about the nice glow of informal warmth that always radiated through their kitchen when they ate dinner together made Carole's appetite disappear.

"I hope you like the chicken, Carole," Mrs. Atwood said. "It's a new recipe for me. I had something like it at the Bradley girl's wedding a few weeks ago, and I thought it was so good, I just had to try to figure out what they'd put on it. I think maybe it could use a little more tarragon."

Carole tried to smile. It wasn't easy when she was feeling so homesick for something as simple as her dad's baked chicken. "Oh, I'm sure this is delicious," Carole said. She picked up her knife and fork and took a bite of her dinner. "Very good," she said, but then she set down her fork.

"I know it's always hard when there's a change in routine," Mrs. Atwood said warmly. Carole understood that Mrs. Atwood was just trying to reassure her. It wasn't working, though. What she felt was lonely, even in this room filled with people she normally liked a lot.

"Oh, Carole," Mr. Atwood said. "I almost forgot to tell you. You had another call from Sergeant Fowler. It seems she had your father on the other line, and she wanted to connect the two of you up so that you could speak to him."

Speak? She could have talked with her dad when she'd been so busy scrolling through the bulletin boards at Stevie's? How could she have missed that?

"Is everything okay with him?" Carole asked. "I mean, did Sergeant Fowler say anything about how he was?"

"It seemed that way to me," said Mr. Atwood. "Sergeant Fowler seemed cheerful and just disappointed for your father that you weren't here. Don't worry, though, dear. I bet he'll try to call again tomorrow and you can talk to him then."

*Maybe*, Carole thought. But then, how many chances could her dad realistically have to call her from the middle of some desert?

Carole took another bite of the chicken and wondered if it would have tasted any better if Mrs. Atwood had added the extra tarragon. No, she decided. Homesick tasted like homesick, no matter how much tarragon you put on it.

"THAT BOOK, *The Arms of Krupp*, is really interesting," Lisa said, handing a pot to Carole to dry. "I just about lost track of time while I was at the library reading it. I guess you must have been doing something as interesting at Stevie's this afternoon."

"Sort of . . . exactly," Carole said, smiling. The fact was that she and Stevie had been doing exactly what Lisa had been doing—research for her paper—only she and Stevie had found it only sort of interesting. "And speaking of that, Stevie and I came across some things on the Internet that you might be able to use. I'll give you the list when we go upstairs."

"Oh, thanks," said Lisa. "Say, did you know . . ."

Carole knew that Lisa was speaking, but she also knew

that she wasn't going to have to listen very closely. It was annoying that she and Stevie had spent some time and effort to get her material that might be helpful and the only response Lisa had for her was "Oh, thanks." She'd probably be more grateful when she saw the actual material, and Carole would give it to her in a moment, but her own disappointment at Lisa's reaction served to make her feel glummer and miss her father more.

Lisa hadn't said a thing about Carole's father, and she hadn't asked one question about Pine Hollow and how the horses were doing. Those were the things that mattered the most to Carole then. The only thing Lisa wanted to talk about was her paper. Sometimes people said that Carole had a one-track mind—that all she ever thought about or wanted to talk about was horses. It was true that she cared about horses, but it wasn't true that that was the only thing she cared about. After all, she and Stevie had spent the whole afternoon trying to do something nice for Lisa, and now Lisa didn't seem to care what they'd done *and* didn't care enough about Carole to ask after the things that mattered to her.

Carole clenched her teeth. She was tired. She was stressed. She was homesick. Maybe Lisa wasn't being fair to her, but maybe Carole wasn't being fair to Lisa, either. She put the final pot in the cabinet, wiped some water off the counter, and told Lisa she was tired.

"It's been another long day for me. I think I'll go do a

little bit of homework and then get to sleep early. I'll see you in the morning."

"Sure. It's okay," Lisa said. "I've got some work to do, too. I brought home some books so that I can start working on my bibliography as well as the research for my paper."

"Good night, Lisa" was all Carole could muster at that point. She put the dish towel on the rack to dry and went on up to her temporary room. The list of books and articles that she and Stevie had assembled from the Internet was on top of her book bag. She walked it across the hall and put it on Lisa's bed, more than a little relieved that Lisa hadn't come upstairs yet. This didn't seem to be a very good time to try any more light conversation with Lisa. It seemed like a very good time to be alone.

On a day when it seemed that few things had gone right, something definitely was going right. The only homework she had was to draw a picture to illustrate the story they'd just read in English class—"The Legend of Sleepy Hollow." The thing Carole was the very best at drawing was, of course, horses. The thing she was worst at drawing was people's heads. The headless horseman was practically a custom-made subject for her. She was finished in no time at all. She then put away her books and slipped into her pajamas. She picked up the Dick Francis book she'd borrowed from the library and slid under the covers to read for a while.

She didn't read for long. She couldn't concentrate at all. As soon as the household was quiet around her and she had finished all her chores, her mind wandered to her father. How could she have missed his phone call?

Carole was certain he'd planned the call to coincide with the time she usually got home from Pine Hollow. He knew she should be home. He wanted to talk with her as much as she wanted to talk with him. She wanted to know he was all right. She also wanted some hint, just a tiny inkling, about where he was. She'd looked through every page of the newspaper at the Lakes' and didn't see anything that would suggest where the country might be sending Marines. She had listened to the radio news broadcast at Pine Hollow and hadn't heard anything there, either. She did realize that her father had said his mission was top secret, and she understood that that made it unlikely the Marines were going to announce to any reporters exactly where they'd sent Colonel Hanson, but she was hoping for a hint. The only thing she knew for sure was that it was out of the country, because her father had taken his passport.

She could almost hear his voice now. "Hi, hon, it's Dad! How are you?"

"I'm fine—now that I've heard from you, anyway."

"Everything okay?"

"Wonderful," she'd say. And she'd mean it, too. Even when she was homesick, worried about him, and worried about the horses, particularly Delilah and Starlight, just being able to talk to her father would make everything wonderful. Without him, it felt as if everything was wrong and there wasn't anything she could do about any of it. She was worried, the horses might be sick—might even die! Lisa was distracted about some dumb history paper that she didn't even have to hand in for six months, and Stevie was more interested in learning about the Underground Railroad than anything else. It felt as if nothing made sense. Nobody was where they were supposed to be. Nothing was going the way it should. Carole's eyelids drifted closed. Before she knew it, she was asleep, and then she was dreaming. Only it wasn't a dream. It was a nightmare.

Carole's father flipped back the flap on the tent and emerged from its dark interior. All around, there was nothing but sand. Gusts of wind picked up clouds of sand and swirled them in eddies like miniature tornadoes. Suddenly a strange, amorphous figure emerged from one of the eddies, or perhaps the eddy turned into this figure.

"Your wish?" it asked Colonel Hanson.

"The camels! Bring the camels!" Carole's father commanded, clapping his hands imperiously.

"But sir, you ask the impossible—"

"Impossible?" Colonel Hanson boomed, his voice echoing across the great, hot emptiness around him.

"They are sick," the spirit said. "They will not be

96

better for forty-five days. And you must be with them. You must stay. Here. Forever."

"But Dad!" Carole said.

He didn't hear her. "Well, if that's the case, then I have to prepare. Men!" he cried out. Marines appeared from all the other tents. "The camels are sick. There is no way for us to get home. We're here for good, so let's make the best of it!"

"But sir, our families!" one young lieutenant cried out.

"For good!" Colonel Hanson repeated.

"Dad!" Carole said.

He still didn't hear her. He never would, and she knew it.

Carole felt the terror fill her whole being. Her eyes welled up. Her world was out of control, and there wasn't anything she could do. Suddenly she sat up, realizing only vaguely that she was in a bed, nowhere near a desert, and nowhere near her father. She shook her head. Her Dick Francis book slid off her chest and onto the floor. The light by her bed was still lit. The clock said 4:00.

Carole sighed. It was only a dream—a nightmare. She was okay. Even knowing that, though, she still felt all the unhappiness in the dream. Perhaps her father wasn't stranded in the desert with a herd of sick camels, but there was too much truth in her feelings to find the facts much more comforting than the nightmare.

She reached for the book and closed it. She turned out the light and pulled up the covers. Maybe her next dream would be a good one.

Across the hall, Lisa wasn't doing much better. The bell rang. Science was over. Time for history class. As she walked down the hall, she saw Fiona Jamieson ahead of her. Fiona was carrying a huge stack of books. Could it be she was working on her next paper, too? What was she reading? Lisa called her name and jogged to catch up with her. Fiona kept walking. Lisa started running. Fiona kept walking. Lisa sprinted. Fiona kept walking. No matter how fast Lisa made herself go, Fiona, steadily walking, was faster.

"*Grrrr*," came a fierce sound. Lisa stopped running. She woke up. Her little Lhasa apso, Dolly, was standing foursquare at the foot of the bed, growling fiercely at Lisa's feet under the covers. With a start, Lisa realized that she'd been having a nightmare. She wasn't really on her way to history class. Fiona wasn't really ahead of her. But apparently she'd really been running—or at least the lying-down equivalent of running. That's what had gotten Dolly so upset.

"It's okay, Dolly. I'm not going to hurt you," Lisa said, patting the little dog affectionately. She glanced at the clock on her bedside table. Four A.M.! It was time to get some restful sleep. No more nightmares!

Dolly settled back down again, and so did Lisa. Restful

sleep. How could she ever get restful sleep if the only thing on her mind was going to be her paper—for the next six months?

"What am I doing?" Lisa asked. Dolly perked up her ears when Lisa spoke, confirming to Lisa that she'd actually said it out loud. *This is crazy,* she thought. *Even at my craziest, I'm not this crazy. I do very well in school. I'm one of the best in school, and I'm proud of it. But I can't let myself get tied up into all these knots. There must be another way.*

She pulled up the covers and put her head back down on the pillow. *Yes, another way,* she thought as she drifted back to sleep.

A FEW HOUSES AWAY, on the second floor, Stevie's room was almost completely dark—almost, that is, if you didn't count the flashlight that glowed dimly through the blankets over Stevie's head. Stevie didn't care what time it was. She didn't want to look at her clock. The only thing she wanted to do was read another chapter, or six, of *The Path to Freedom.* No matter how tired she was in the morning, it would be worth it—worth every yawn, just to have read some more of this truly great book.

Now, where was she? *Oh, yes,* she thought. Hallie had just met the man who had given her something to drink. No, that was someone else. Hallie was about to see if the pony in the field could carry— No, that wasn't a pony, that was a horse, and it belonged to the man who had been angry with the man who had given her a drink. Or did it belong to the man who had given her a drink? Stevie refocused the flashlight on the page she'd been reading. She rubbed her eyes and looked hard at the page. The letters merged with one another. The words started to swim. Stevie couldn't read them at all! There was something wrong with the book! How could she find out the end of Hallie's nightmarish journey with Esther if the book was all messed up?

She shoved the covers back and focused the flashlight on her clock. There was something wrong with the clock, too! It said it was after four o'clock in the morning. That was impossible! Stevie pointed the light at her wristwatch. It said exactly the same thing.

She knew then that there was nothing wrong with the clock or the book. There was something wrong with her head. The reason the words were all messed up on the page was that her eyes were all messed up in her head. They wanted to sleep! Staying up all night to read wasn't a smart move, especially on a school night. She clicked off the flashlight, put the book on her bedside table, and closed her eyes.

"I'll finish it tomor . . . ," she muttered to her darkened room. She didn't finish the word, however. She was already asleep.

13

"I'M TOTALLY BEAT," Carole confided to Lisa and Stevie when the three of them met up at Pine Hollow the next afternoon.

"Me too," Lisa said. "I had this awful dream last night."

"Maybe you had the same one I had," said Carole. "Was it in a desert?"

"No, in school," Lisa said.

"I thought *I* was the one who had nightmares about school," said Stevie.

"Well, you *look* as if you'd had a nightmare," Carole teased.

"I didn't. I was just reading about one. It's this great book, see—"

"I know, I know, *The Path to Freedom*, by Elizabeth Wallingford Johnson," Carole supplied. She'd heard a lot about that book over the past few days.

"You're going to love it, both of you," Stevie said.

"You already told us," said Lisa.

It was easy to chat with her friends most of the time, Carole thought. And it was good to chat with them, too. When the three of them were together, things seemed to go right, especially when what they were talking about or doing had to do with horses. Today they weren't talking about horses, yet, but they were about to ride them.

Each of them was acutely aware that a large dark cloud hung over Pine Hollow and would for a considerable period. It wasn't going to help to talk about it. Very soon they'd start getting some of the blood tests back. Then, if everything was okay, maybe they could talk about it. Now, however, it was best to chat about books and nightmares they'd slept through rather than diseases and nightmares they might have to live through.

"Class begins in fifteen minutes!" Mrs. Reg announced over the PA system. That didn't give the girls much time. They dropped their books in their cubbies, yanked on their riding clothes and boots, and ran to the tack room to get saddles and bridles for their horses.

"Last one at the good-luck horseshoe is a rotten egg!" Stevie declared.

Twelve minutes later all three girls met at the horseshoe. Stevie was the closest to it. Lisa and Carole were right next to each other.

"So who's the rotten egg if there's a tie?" Stevie asked.

Lisa and Carole decided to be much too cool to race each other.

"Very childish," said Lisa in a superior voice.

"Definitely," Carole agreed with a sniff. Both girls grinned at Stevie.

"You can both be rotten eggs," Stevie suggested. "But if you guys are both rotten eggs and I'm not, I won't have any fun. So let's all be rotten eggs."

The three girls touched the horseshoe together and then rode into the ring.

It was fun to be able to joke about things like rotten eggs with her friends, but Stevie knew, and she knew that both Lisa and Carole knew, that what was really on their minds that afternoon wasn't rotten eggs. It was swamp fever.

They'd all sensed a tension at Pine Hollow the minute they'd arrived. The place was not the usual beehive of activity. There were no vans pulling in, no horses being loaded or unloaded. There was a notice on the door of the stable explaining the reason for and terms of the quarantine.

Everyone looked at the horses with an awful curiosity. Were they okay now? Would they stay that way? The facts of EIA were known to everyone. It was a dreadful, deadly disease. It could sweep through a stable and destroy every horse in the place. Could that happen at their beloved Pine Hollow?

Stevie leaned forward and patted Belle's neck while they walked around the ring to warm up before class started. She often did that as a means of thanking Belle for something she'd done. Today it was more a matter of thanking her for just being. Belle was the most perfect horse Stevie could ever imagine herself riding. She could barely consider what it might be like if something—and she couldn't even say the name of the disease to herself—happened to her beloved Belle.

"Class, come to order," Max said. The students all lined up in the middle of the ring and faced him. They waited for his instructions.

"Today we're going to work on balance exercises." He explained how each rider would try to be in balance not just on her horse, but with her horse. "If you visualize yourself as a part of the horse, not just a body plopped onto the back of the horse, it will be easier to find your balance with the horse," he said.

"That's just what I've always wanted to be, anyway!" Carole said. The other riders smiled. Some even laughed.

Normally Max would frown or even get annoyed when riders called out in class. Today he just smiled at Carole's joke. That was when Carole realized that Max was as edgy as the riders. That was a little comforting, confirming Carole's feeling that they were all in this together—not just three rotten eggs, but a whole class-ful, plus the teacher.

"Okay, now start walking around the ring, and when I call out gaits, change not only the gait, but your sense of balance with the horse. That means that your horse isn't the only one that's walking, trotting, or cantering. You have to be doing it, too. You're not being pulled along or carried by the horse. You are riding it."

*Walk, walk, walk,* Lisa said to herself, trying to sense that her own body was moving in union with Prancer's. Most of the time, this wasn't a difficult exercise for her. She naturally felt, and responded to, the horse's move-ments. Her balance was always good. Max had often said that she was naturally graceful in the saddle. Lisa thought that was partly from years of classes in ballet, in which balance was also critically important.

"Lisa, you've got to sit up straighter," Max said. "Meg, your hands are wiggling. Hold them still. Stevie, what are your heels doing up? Put them down. Betsy, look where you want the horse to go, not at your friends—not even at me. Carole, there should be a single straight line from your elbows, through your wrists and hands, along the reins to Starlight's mouth—not the zigzag thing I'm seeing now."

Carole looked down at her arms. She couldn't believe what she'd been doing, any more than she could believe that Lisa wasn't sitting straight and that Stevie's heels were up. These were beginners' mistakes! What was the matter with them? Meg knew better than to wiggle her hands. And everybody knew you should be looking in the direction you wanted the horse to go.

"All right, now, starting with Polly, I want you to cut across the ring and change directions to circle clockwise."

Polly Giacomin looked at him, confused. "Max, we're already going clockwise."

"Well, then, counterclockwise," he said, a little flustered.

Now even Max was making beginners' mistakes! Then Carole understood. Everybody, including her and including Max, was nervous. They were all doing things they never did normally.

Then Mrs. Reg did something she never did normally. She came into the ring and interrupted the class. When she went to speak to Max, all the riders stopped, watched, and waited.

Max noticed the audience. "Why don't you tell them?" he said to his mother.

"We've just had a call from Judy Barker," Mrs. Reg said. "She's gotten the results of the Coggins test for the first half of the horses. They are all negative."

"Delilah?" Carole asked.

"Not yet," said Mrs. Reg. "Her blood sample was in the second set. We'll probably hear about that tomorrow. But so far, so good!"

"Yahoo!" Stevie cried out joyfully. She was joined by

all the other students. Max smiled at the spontaneous celebration, but he had a note of caution for the students.

"It's good news, but it's not great news," he reminded them soberly. "The only way any of the horses here would be infected and have a positive test at this point would be if there were a widespread epidemic going on, and nobody ever suspected that. Remember, Delilah had only been back for a day, so if she's infected and has infected any of the other horses in the stable, the earliest that could possibly show up in a blood test is about ten days from now. We didn't expect any of our other horses to test positive at this time. The real test will be at the end of the quarantine period—in forty-three days. Now, cross your stirrups over your saddles and take up a sitting trot, counterclockwise. Polly, you begin."

After class, the three girls cross-tied their horses in the aisle of the stable so that they could groom and talk at the same time. It seemed like the best they could do for a Saddle Club meeting that day, since Lisa had an appointment to get to and Stevie needed to hurry home for something. She wasn't saying what, but based on the circles under her eyes, Carole hoped it was for some sleep.

"You know, I've always known that we were three of the luckiest girls in the world," Carole said. "I mean, we've got each other and we've got horses. What more could anyone want?"

"To have the horses stay healthy," said Stevie.

"Forever," added Lisa.

"Exactly what I had in mind," Carole agreed. "And to think that the whole thing could be wrecked by one little deerfly and one tiny virus."

"I don't want to think about it," Stevie declared. "For now, everything is fine, and what we don't know about the future can't hurt us."

"I sort of agree," Lisa said. "I mean, we all know the realities here. It's possible that some horses have been infected, but there's no point in looking for trouble. So far, so good. I'm happy to leave it that way."

"Me too," said Stevie.

"I guess," Carole said. But was that realistic? Weren't there things they could be doing? She had a nagging feeling but decided not to share it with her friends yet.

Lisa glanced at her watch and then finished up her grooming very quickly. "I've got to go," she said.

"I'll put Prancer back in her stall," Carole offered. Lisa accepted and ran off. When Stevie looked at her watch, too, Carole knew she was in a hurry as well. "And Belle," she said.

"Thanks," said Stevie, and then she was gone.

Carole finished grooming Starlight, gave him a big hug and two carrots, and then put all three horses back in their stalls. She gave Belle and Prancer carrots, too.

It was only five-thirty. She didn't have to rush back to the Atwoods', and she had some unfinished business.

She wanted to visit Delilah and see how she was getting along in her lonely splendor.

Carole said it that way to herself, but even as she was walking over to the feed shed, she knew that wasn't what she'd meant. She wanted to spend some time with Delilah to see if she was showing any symptoms. Would she be hungry today? Would her ears perk up when Carole walked in? Was she in any pain? In short, was she showing any symptoms of illness? Carole practically held her breath as she opened the door.

Delilah stood at the back of her temporary stall. She looked warily at the door as it opened—almost a glare rather than a look. Carole was sure something was wrong. She walked slowly to the mare and held out her hand to pat her. Naturally friendly and welcoming, Delilah would normally walk up to greet a visitor. Today she remained aloof.

Carole slipped into the stall, latching the door behind her. She moved slowly, wary of upsetting the uneasy horse. She looked around. Horses often had symptoms of illness around them as well as in them. Carole saw several of them. First of all, Delilah hadn't finished the grain she'd been given at breakfast. Loss of appetite was common in many equine illnesses. Her water bucket was also full, but Carole had no way of knowing when it had last been filled. There seemed to be less manure in the stall than she would have expected at this time of day, confirming that Delilah hadn't been eating very much.

Delilah was definitely not feeling very good. Her eyes seemed a little dull, and she was nervous.

Carole reached for her halter and held it securely. Delilah didn't pull away, but she didn't come to Carole. When Carole reached her, she patted the mare. Delilah liked that. For the first time since Carole had entered the shed, she felt that Delilah was, in fact, glad to have her there. Carole couldn't help herself. She hugged Delilah. The mare liked that, too. She nickered softly over Carole's shoulder.

Carole stepped back and regarded the mare carefully. It wasn't clear that Delilah was really sick. It was just clear to Carole that she wasn't really well. Should she call Judy, as she had with Nero the other day?

What if Judy told her that Delilah was sick—really sick? What if she had gotten EIA from King Perry? Carole didn't want to hear that from Judy or anybody. She wouldn't call Judy, now or ever!

Carole handed Delilah a piece of carrot. Delilah took it and chewed slowly. That seemed like pretty good news. While Delilah chomped on the carrot, Carole returned to the stall door, climbed up the boards, and perched on top of it. She could watch Delilah from there, and she could think.

Carole remembered when Delilah had carried her first foal, Samson, son of Cobalt—when Carole and her friends had helped bring him into the world, when he'd taken his first steps, when Delilah had licked him clean, lovingly, and then had given him his first meal. And now this new foal . . . Was there one? Was it possible that Delilah was simply suffering from some kind of morning sickness? *Maybe*, Carole thought. *Maybe*. Then she decided to stop thinking. She had to do something instead.

She hopped down off the stall door and rummaged around in the feed area until she found a jar of molasses. Horses were famous for liking sweet things, and Carole was pretty sure that if she sweetened up the remaining grain in Delilah's feed box, she'd finish up her breakfast. A mare carrying a foal had to eat well because she was eating for two. Carole poured several tablespoons of the thick, sticky liquid into Delilah's leftovers, stirred it with a spoon, and then put some of the concoction on her fingers and took it over to Delilah.

The horse sniffed curiously. She couldn't resist it. Her soft, warm lips opened up and gathered the treat into her mouth. That made Carole feel good.

She left the stall then, latching the door carefully behind her, and washed her hands.

"Bye-bye, girl," Carole said. "I'll stop in again tomorrow."

As she closed the feed shed door behind her, Carole heard Delilah whicker at her softly. That made her smile. She felt better now than when she'd first gone in.

She'd done everything she could for the mare, hadn't she?

# 14

"TWO-THIRDS OF a Saddle Club meeting in my room in five minutes!" Lisa declared. Dinner was over, and the girls had gone upstairs to get ready for the night and then do their homework. Now it sounded as if Lisa wanted to have a little fun, too, rather than just sticking her nose in her books all night long. That would be a welcome change for Carole.

This evening had been a big improvement over last night for Carole at the Atwoods'. For one thing, she had been on time tonight. She'd helped make the dinner and she'd helped clean up. She'd even been able to eat some of it. She definitely felt better about being a houseguest tonight than she had the night before. She just wished that everything else was moving ahead in such a satisfactory manner.

Four minutes later she had slipped into her pajamas and was knocking on Lisa's door.

"C'mon in!" Lisa said cheerfully. While Carole was feeling somewhat better, clearly Lisa was feeling a lot better, and that was a relief—for both of them.

Carole sat cross-legged on Lisa's bed and took the cookie Lisa offered her.

"So, did you reach Sergeant Fowler this afternoon?" Lisa asked.

Carole nodded and then swallowed her first bite of cookie. "I called her from Pine Hollow because I wanted to make sure I caught her before she left. She said Dad probably wouldn't call again for a couple of days, but he really was fine and cheerful. Even she didn't know where he was, but he didn't seem concerned about anything at all, except, of course, for not being able to reach me."

"Well, that's great," Lisa said. "So now you know he's really all right."

"I guess so," said Carole. "But it did cross my mind that if something were wrong, if he weren't all right or if he were afraid that something might go wrong, he probably wouldn't tell Sergeant Fowler and she definitely wouldn't tell me."

"Oh, right," said Lisa. "Still, you know she talked

with him and he didn't sound worried or anything, right?"

"I guess," said Carole. Then, wanting to change the subject, she asked Lisa where she'd hurried off to that afternoon.

"My therapist," said Lisa. "I still go, you know."

"Right," said Carole, a little sorry she'd asked the question. It wasn't that Lisa was secretive about the fact that she was getting therapy, it was that Carole and Stevie never asked her about it because they figured if there was anything she wanted them to know, she'd tell. Now Carole had blundered right into it and asked the question she hadn't meant to ask. Lisa didn't seem to mind, however. In fact, she seemed more than a little eager to share some of what had gone on.

"I told her all about Fiona, about the paper, and about how you guys were helping me with it."

"Was that okay?" Carole asked.

"Of course," said Lisa. "And, speaking of that, I don't think I did a very good job of thanking you and Stevie for giving me that information from her computer."

"It was helpful stuff?"

"Definitely," Lisa said. "But I don't really think I need it quite yet."

"We just wanted to save you some time," Carole said, shrugging off their efforts.

"No, I don't mean it that way," said Lisa. "I mean that

the more I talked about this with Susan, the more I could see her eyes opening wide. She doesn't normally get upset about stuff I tell her, but this time she made an exception. She was almost angry with me. When I stop to think about it, I don't know why you and Stevie weren't angry with me, too."

"No, we weren't angry," Carole told her. "Just worried. That's why we wanted to help you."

"Well, Susan wanted to help me, too. She said there really isn't any difference, as far as a computer is concerned, between an A and an A-plus. If I do the best I can and become valedictorian, fine. If Fiona does, well, she can have it. And if we both do best, then we can be co-valedictorians."

"I see her point," Carole said.

Lisa picked up another cookie and took a bite before going on.

"Well, I could see her point, too, but of course it doesn't make any sense at all if you look at it carefully. Being a co-valedictorian is useless. There is something known as 'best,' and two people can't be 'best.' 'Best' is what I've always expected to be. You know that. So I don't really have a choice."

Carole was getting a bad feeling about this. What was Lisa leading up to?

"If I can't be best, at least I have to know why, and the only way I can know why is if I'm in control. I've made the decision now. I've decided to let Fiona go ahead and be the valedictorian. I am going to get a C in history."

*"What?"* Carole asked. This was more confused than she could have imagined.

"A C," Lisa repeated. "You've heard of them, haven't you? It's the grade average students get. I think it's time for me to show that I'm not obsessing about my grade point average, but I'm still in control. I'll be very proud of my C."

Carole nearly choked on her final bite of chocolate chip cookie. The idea of Lisa's getting an intentional C in a course was totally bizarre. She'd nearly gone out of her mind when she'd gotten an unintentional B+ in math last year! It had been as if it was the end of her academic career. Good-bye to Harvard! Farewell Rhodes scholarship!

Carole couldn't say what was on her mind. In the first place, if she tried to talk, she was going to spurt chocolate chip cookie all over the place, because there was no way she could swallow while she was thinking about Lisa getting a C. In the second place, if she hadn't been angry with Lisa before, she certainly was now, and she strongly suspected that it would be bad for their friendship if she told Lisa what she actually thought of this new plan.

"Interesting," Carole said when she could finally talk.

"Yes, I think so. And speaking of interesting, what is going on with Stevie?" Lisa asked.

"Beats me," said Carole. "But she looked awful today—like she'd gotten about three hours of sleep."

"Do you think something's worrying her?" Lisa asked.

"I don't know. She's usually more forthcoming about what's on her mind, especially when she's got a problem. So maybe we have to pry a little bit to see what's going on."

"Sounds like a Saddle Club project to me," said Lisa.

"Yes, we should see if we can figure out what's on her mind. Actually, there's something I want to talk with her about anyway. I'll call her a little later and see if I can get any information, so we'll know what we're dealing with here."

"Good idea. And it's good if you call her, too. Because even if I'm going to get a C in history, I've still got a lot of irregular French verbs to memorize. One C will be enough for me this semester."

"Right," Carole said, standing up. "I'll get to work, too. See you in the morning."

As soon as Carole left the room, Lisa headed for her telephone. It suited her fine that Carole was going to call Stevie later, because Lisa was going to call her now. Carole was in trouble, and she and Stevie had to do something about it!

A dopey-sounding Stevie came to the phone.

"H'lo?" she said.

117

"Did I wake you up?" Lisa asked. She looked at her watch. It was just eight-thirty!

"Um, I don't remember," Stevie mumbled into the phone.

There were a few similar exchanges of senseless conversation before Lisa could get Stevie turned in the right direction. Lisa had been talking with Carole about Stevie, but she was more concerned about Carole.

"We've got to do something for Carole," Lisa said. "She's in trouble!"

"Trouble?" asked Stevie. She was awake and alert now.

"Trouble," Lisa confirmed. "I think she's so worried about her father that she's letting absolutely everything drive her wild. I mean, she missed his call last night, and tonight she talked with Sergeant Fowler, who said everything was fine, but Carole doesn't believe her!"

"Oh no," said Stevie. "Any good reason for her not to believe Sergeant Fowler?"

"Not that I can see," said Lisa. "It's as if Carole's decided she's going to worry no matter what anyone tells her. And you know Carole. When she starts worrying senselessly, she can start doing the oddest things. We've got to find a way to let her know that everything's fine with her father."

"Maybe we should call Sergeant Fowler," suggested Stevie.

"That's exactly what I had in mind," Lisa said. "And

118

you're the person to do it. You're the best person I know at convincing adults to do something they don't necessarily know they ought to be doing, and you'll have to talk her into getting Colonel Hanson to call at a time when we know Carole will be home and can talk to him."

"And who's going to convince him to tell Carole that he's okay in a way she'll believe?" Stevie asked.

It sometimes surprised Lisa when her friends were more logical than she was, but she had to admit that Stevie had asked a good question.

"We'll come up with something," said Lisa.

It sometimes surprised Stevie when her friends were more illogical than she was, but Lisa was right. They would come up with something, somehow.

"Now, can I go back to bed?" Stevie asked.

"Sure," Lisa said. She didn't think it was a good idea to mention that Carole would be calling her later that night.

"I CALLED STEVIE last night, but Chad answered and said she was sound asleep—at nine o'clock!" Carole told Lisa the following morning. The two of them were sitting at the breakfast table. Carole was eating a bowl of cereal. Lisa was having toast and a glass of juice. Normally Mrs. Atwood made breakfast for the family. This morning, however, both Lisa and Carole had awakened very early. It wasn't even seven o'clock yet, and they were both dressed and hungry.

"I guess she really was tired yesterday," said Lisa, sipping her orange juice.

"Just like we may be tonight because of getting up so early! Say, what woke you up?" Carole asked.

"Oh, I guess my determination to follow through on

my new plan," said Lisa. "I'm excited about it. It's so daring! Anyway, I want to get to school early so that I can do some work in the computer lab."

"Oh," said Carole. Then she thought that in the whole wide world, it would only be Lisa Atwood who would need to get to school extra early in order to get a poor grade. Carole decided to keep that thought to herself. "Well, as long as you're leaving early, I'll leave with you," she said. "There's something I want to check in the library."

"Good," said Lisa. "I like to have company walking to school."

They didn't talk much as they walked. It was so early that both of them were still a little dozy. The streets and sidewalks of Lisa's neighborhood were empty except for the occasional commuter headed for the train station. There were no clusters of children waiting for buses or mothers herding students into cars. That would all happen an hour later. For now, the town was a slightly different world from what either Carole or Lisa was accustomed to.

"See you at lunch," Lisa said, waving cheerfully to Carole as she headed for the computer lab. Carole hung her jacket in her locker and stowed her book bag there until her first class. She didn't need her books for her errand in the library.

The librarian looked up and greeted Carole as she came in. She was always there early for any students who wanted or needed to be at school early. This morning, there weren't any other students in the library. Carole smiled back. She didn't need any help. She knew where to look.

She went to the fiction section for older readers and walked along the shelf until she came to the J's. There it was, *The Path to Freedom* by Elizabeth Wallingford Johnson. Carole was curious about the book. She was curious because the Underground Railroad was a subject that interested her, but she was more curious because the book seemed to have a sort of hold on Stevie. Stevie would give her her own copy to read when she'd finished it, and that wouldn't be too long. In the meantime, though, Carole wanted to get a head start. Maybe it would cast some light on what was going on in Stevie's head. Between Lisa and Stevie, Carole would have preferred to understand what was going on in Lisa's head. The glimpse she'd had last night, however, had convinced her that it was too weird for her to be able to understand. She had a better shot at Stevie's head. Stevie could be weird, for sure, but there was always a pleasantly twisted logic to her weirdness.

She took the book off the shelf and settled down on the big, comfortable sofa to read. She had forty-five minutes before the bell. That was enough to get some insight. At least she hoped it was.

She was on page fourteen when she became aware that someone else had come into the library. The other person was clicking furiously at the keys of the computer catalog, making notes, printing out lists. It was eager, excited activity, hard for Carole to ignore, and when the other person said, "Oh, wow!" Carole looked up.

It was none other than Fiona Jamieson, and Carole was sure she was working on the bibliography for her history paper—due in six months. What was the matter with these people?

"Fiona?" Carole said.

The girl set the computer to work on another search and then turned around in her chair. "Oh, hi. Carole, isn't it?" They weren't in the same class, so it wasn't surprising that Fiona wasn't sure who she was.

"Right. Carole Hanson," Carole confirmed. "What are you doing here at this hour?" Carole hoped she sounded friendly rather than accusatory, which was how she felt.

"Oh, I'm just looking up some stuff," said Fiona.

*Of course she's just looking up some stuff,* thought Carole. *That's what people do on a computer catalog.* "Got a paper coming up?" she asked.

"Not really," said Fiona. "I mean, I do, but it doesn't have to be done for months. I just like to get ahead on my reading. I feel better when I do that, and I know I learn a lot more if I'm prepared for the classes."

That made sense to Carole.

"So what are you doing here?" Fiona asked.

"Just reading a book someone recommended," said

123

Carole. "It's about the Underground Railroad. I've just started it, though."

"Oh, *The Path to Freedom*? I read that. It's really good. You'll love it. It's got this wonderful, authentic feel to it—like you're right there with Hallie."

"That's what I heard," said Carole.

The computer beeped, informing Fiona that her search was complete. She turned back to the screen. Carole turned her eyes back to her book, but her attention was on Fiona.

Fiona seemed very normal—not at all the apple-polishing goody-goody Lisa made her out to be. Fiona was interested in what she was studying and wanted to know more than she could get from the textbook. That seemed admirable to Carole, not despicable, as Lisa found it. Clearly, Lisa was viewing Fiona solely as competition, just the way she sometimes thought of her grades as contest results. Winning was what mattered.

From what Carole had seen so far, Lisa could stand to take a page out of Fiona's book. It wasn't going to do any good to suggest that to Lisa. Lisa would have to learn it herself. Choosing to get a C was no more the answer than choosing to work herself to death to get an A+.

Then Fiona stood up from the computer and hurried over to the shelves. Carole watched surreptitiously while Fiona's eyes scanned the shelf for the book she wanted. She pulled a book out, flipped it open to the index, and then turned to a page near the middle.

"Great!" she said. It was an involuntary utterance, just as the earlier "Wow" had been. This was a girl who really loved to learn, Carole thought. She found it almost inspirational.

"Found something interesting?" Carole asked.

"Definitely!" Fiona responded. "Extra credit, I'm sure! I'm trying to study up on the German economy between the wars, and there's enough material here and in some of these other books for me to do a whole project on it. If I can get some extra credit, I'm sure to get an A-plus, and I really want that. Isn't it great?"

Carole's heart sank. She'd misread Fiona completely. The girl was as nuts as Lisa. Maybe more. Lisa hadn't been considering extra credit!

Carole couldn't contain herself anymore. She loved Lisa so much that she could hold her tongue for her, but Fiona wasn't her best friend, so she couldn't curb her feelings. They flooded her and then burst out.

"I've had enough of this stuff!" she declared angrily. "Do you really think school and grades are just a contest? What's important here is what you can learn and how much you can enjoy it and what it all means to you as an individual! What difference does it make if a piece of paper says you're really good at school or really, *really* good at school? The only thing that matters in school or anyplace is whether you've done the best you can. Being better than someone else doesn't matter at all!"

125

Fiona looked at Carole, stunned. This was a girl Fiona barely knew, and she was giving her a lecture on the meaning of school and life! Carole wasn't finished, either.

"Do you have any idea how it feels to be utterly helpless in a situation? Do you know what it means when you can't solve a problem by getting extra credit—or what it means to fail completely? It's time for some people to learn that life isn't just about things you can control with your obsessions! It's about things that control you, too!"

With that, Carole stood up from the sofa, placed her book on the return shelf, and walked out, leaving behind an astonished history student.

Her own words echoed in her mind. She meant them. She wasn't sorry she'd said them. She was, however, surprised at how much she'd revealed to herself. Helpless, out of control, failing. Yes, that was exactly how she felt. Briefly she wished she could get some extra credit at life, bring her father home, and heal all the sick horses. It didn't work that way, though, and she knew it.

# 16

OUT OF CONTROL. That was the way Carole was feeling, and that was the way her world felt. There was no better way to describe it. She'd realized that when she was speaking to Fiona, and nothing that had happened all day long at school had made her feel any better.

Even now, done with school for the day and on her way to Pine Hollow, she didn't think anything was looking up. Nothing, and she meant nothing, was going the way she wanted it to.

In the first place, there was Lisa, totally weirded out—first by her compulsion to win and then by her compulsion to lose. Next came Stevie. She was behaving weirdly, too. Even though weird was pretty normal for Stevie, she was unusually weird, and she was exhausted.

Something was up, and Carole had no idea what it was or what she could do about it. Next, even though the Atwoods were trying hard to make her feel at home, she didn't really feel at home because it wasn't home. She was always comfortable at Lisa's house, as long as she knew she could go to her own home. This time she couldn't, and that made her think of the things she really couldn't control, things that were distressing her the most.

Her father first. Where was he? What was he up to? Why couldn't they ever talk to one another? She missed him desperately, but most of all, she was worried about him. And then there were all the horses at Pine Hollow. When Carole closed her eyes, she saw rows and rows of empty stalls, an entire stable wiped out by a dreadful disease. EIA, swamp fever—whatever it was called, it was spelled *d-e-a-t-h*.

Carole walked faster, hurrying to Pine Hollow. She had to be there; she had to help her beloved horses. Sure, only one was hers in the legal sense, but they were all beloved in every single sense. There had to be something she could control in the nightmare that was called her life these days.

She'd been walking so fast that she got to Pine Hollow before any of the other schoolkids did. Lisa wasn't coming this afternoon. She'd said she had something else she had to do after school. Stevie wasn't planning to come, either, though Carole couldn't remember if she'd

128

said what it was she was doing. Other riders would show up. They always did, but they weren't there yet. Carole felt as if maybe she was the only one in the world who remembered that Judy was supposed to call this afternoon with the results of the blood tests for all the rest of the horses in the stable—including Delilah.

Carole dropped her book bag and jacket in her cubby and hurried out to the stalls. They were all full. Her nightmare of empty stalls had been just that: a nightmare.

The stable had horses in it, but there were no people. Mrs. Reg was in her office. She and Max were going over papers and were so engrossed in them that they barely waved to Carole. She knew they'd tell her if there was any news from Judy. Then Carole remembered. This was the day Judy worked at CARL, the County Animal Rescue League. There wouldn't be any news from her until she got home—after six o'clock.

Carole hurried to Starlight's stall. Starlight greeted her warmly, nuzzling her neck. He was so sweet and wonderful that Carole wished she could thank her father again, right then and there, for giving Starlight to her. She checked Starlight's water and hay and saw that both supplies had been replenished recently. His stall was clean, too, so there wasn't any work for Carole to do there—except, of course, to hug him and give him a carrot, which she did.

She checked on Belle and Prancer. Obviously, Red

129

had had a busy day, because their stalls were clean as well.

With an uncomfortable feeling, Carole realized that maybe Red wasn't so busy. He had extra time because business was slow at Pine Hollow. Without any horses coming and going and with some riders staying away, even if they didn't have to, the place was quiet. There was plenty of time to do chores all day long.

It felt odd to be at Pine Hollow with nothing to do. She wasn't planning to ride that day, so she'd counted on chores to keep her mind off all the things it seemed to want to think about. There had to be something she could do.

Of course. She could check on Delilah. The sunshine of the autumn afternoon warmed her back as she walked to the feed shed. Carole was oblivious to it. All she could think of was Delilah—lovely, kind, sweet, gentle, motherly Delilah. Carole's hand trembled when she reached for the doorknob to enter the feed shed. What would she find? Would it be the frisky, curious mare she loved, or would she find more symptoms of the disease she didn't even want to think about?

Being afraid wasn't going to solve anything. Carole opened the door and stepped in.

Delilah was sick. She lifted her head to greet Carole, but there was no eagerness, as if she didn't have any to share. Someone who didn't know Delilah might not see it as quickly as Carole did. Most people saw Delilah's beautiful coat and silvery mane long before they saw anything else about her. Delilah's coat and mane were as beautiful as they always were. And although there were horses who always looked at visitors dully, Delilah wasn't one of them.

Carole hurried over to the mare. Delilah lifted her head over the gate to her stall, waiting for the loving greeting she knew she'd get from Carole. Carole held her ever so gently, afraid she might make something hurt, but the horse wasn't in pain and clearly wanted a good hug—the kind she usually got from Carole. Carole delivered. As she did, however, she became aware that Delilah felt very warm.

Carole had always thought her father was being silly when he'd kiss her on the forehead and then tell her he thought she might be coming down with something.

"Oh, Daddy," she'd say.

"Well, you feel warm to me, baby," he'd tell her. "You feeling okay?"

"I feel fine," she'd tell him.

"Go get me the thermometer," he'd tell her. The thermometer almost always agreed with her father, and Carole almost always spent the next couple of days in bed, recovering.

This time, she didn't have to get the thermometer any more than her father did. She knew from holding her that Delilah had a fever.

Carole stepped back and took a look at Delilah. Nothing she saw gave her comfort. The mare's legs seemed puffy, and the skin around her eyes seemed pale. Carole checked Delilah's mouth. Her cheeks and gums seemed paler than usual, too.

*EIA* stood for *equine infectious anemia*. If Carole remembered correctly, anemia was a condition that affected blood so that there wasn't enough iron in it. Blood that wasn't working right wouldn't be able to carry extra fluids around the body properly. Fluids could end up staying in the places that were farthest from a horse's heart—like the lower legs. And blood without enough iron in it wouldn't be the same color as regular blood. It would be pale—like Delilah's gums.

Carole didn't have to wait for a blood test. There was no need to worry about a phone call. She had the answer. Delilah was sick. She was *very* sick, and what she had was the same disease that had killed King Perry only a few days before. They might have been infected at the same time when Delilah first arrived at Hedgerow Farms, or Delilah might have been infected by a tabanid that had just bitten King Perry. They might never know exactly how it had happened, but Carole was as sure as anything that it had happened. Delilah had swamp fever.

She couldn't die, though. She was carrying a foal—King Perry's foal. She had to live. She had to have this foal, and it had to be perfect, just like its brother, Samson. If people thought Delilah was sick, they wouldn't take care of her. They might even euthanize her.

The thought took Carole's breath away. This beautiful horse—gone. Maybe even worse was the idea that she might be separated from all the other horses for the rest of her life. She'd never be ridden again. She'd never jump, she'd never turn on the forehand, enjoy the deep peace of the hilly woods of Virginia. Nobody would ever love her as much as they did before she became ill.

Carole couldn't let that happen to her beloved Delilah. This horse was born to love, to be loved, to be ridden, to be free, happy, cared for. If nobody else would do it for her, Carole would.

"I'll be right back," she told Delilah.

Carole knew what she was going to do, but she didn't have a plan. She only knew she was going to be with Delilah, to love her and look after her as nobody else could. Carole would give her health and strength. They would be together. It was all Delilah would need; it was all Carole would need.

Max and Mrs. Reg were still in the office as Carole slipped into the locker area and put on her riding clothes and boots. There was no sign of Red anywhere, and there was nobody in the tack room. Carole picked up Delilah's saddle and bridle, took a crop, fastened her own helmet under her chin, and headed for the feed shed.

Delilah didn't protest at all while Carole tacked her up, and it only took a minute. Carole tugged gently at the bridle, and Delilah willingly followed her out of the shed. Delilah sniffed at the fresh, cool autumn air. It seemed to energize her. She nodded appreciatively. Carole mounted her, adjusted the stirrups, and headed toward the gate to the field and the woods beyond.

As Carole and Delilah left Pine Hollow, two thoughts crossed Carole's mind. First, she vaguely heard the ring of the stable telephone and wondered if that was the call from Judy. It didn't matter when the call came. Carole was with Delilah, and she would take care of her.

Her other thought was to remember that she hadn't touched the good-luck horseshoe.

17

"WELL, WHAT'LL WE do now?" Lisa asked Stevie.

"Wait, I guess," Stevie said. Waiting wasn't her favorite activity by a long shot, but there didn't seem to be much choice. The two of them stood, side by side, at Lisa's house, glowering at the telephone.

It had seemed like a great plan. The two girls had met at Lisa's after school. Their idea had been to call Sergeant Fowler and explain to her that Carole really, really, *really* needed to talk to her father. It wasn't that there was anything wrong, but Carole seemed to think there were things wrong and was very upset at having missed her father's earlier call.

They were convinced that Sergeant Fowler would understand and would find a way to get word to Colonel

135

Hanson to call at a specific time. They'd decided on eight o'clock that night. Carole had been so upset about being late for dinner that she was sure to be on time; it was a guarantee that she'd be there half an hour after dinner started. Mrs. Atwood didn't normally let Lisa take calls while they were eating, but they were sure she would make an exception if Carole's father called from a top secret place.

Stevie had just found Sergeant Fowler's telephone number and had been about to pick up the phone when it rang. It was Sergeant Fowler calling Carole. Was Carole going to miss another call from her father?

Not if they could help it. Sergeant Fowler had explained that she'd talked to Colonel Hanson that afternoon.

"He's fine," she'd said. "And I know that you believe me when I tell you that, but I also know that no matter what I say, Carole won't believe he's fine until she hears it from her father himself."

"I couldn't have said that better," Lisa had told her.

"So what I've done is to arrange for him to call her this afternoon, in exactly half an hour. She'll be there, right?"

"If it's humanly possible, she'll be here," Lisa had said.

"Good," said Sergeant Fowler. "The colonel has gotten permission to let his family—in this case, Carole—know where he is. She can't tell anyone, so I can't tell you, but once she knows where he is, I am sure she'll feel reassured of his safety. So now, the really important thing is to be sure she's there to take the call—in, um, twenty-eight minutes."

"Aye-aye, ma'am," Lisa'd said, looking at her own watch.

"Thanks, Lisa," Sergeant Fowler had said, and then they'd hung up.

As soon as they'd gotten off the phone, Lisa had called Pine Hollow. It was a sure bet that when Carole wasn't home, she was at Pine Hollow. Lisa was glad, for once, that Carole was so totally predictable!

The phone had rung and rung. It had rung eight times before Mrs. Reg had picked it up. She'd seemed a little annoyed. Lisa knew she'd interrupted something and had apologized, but she explained that she was looking for Carole because her father was going to phone.

Mrs. Reg had called out Carole's name. No answer. Max had looked around the stable. Carole wasn't there. Mrs. Reg had vaguely remembered seeing her there earlier, but had assured them she wasn't there now and that Starlight was in his stall, so Carole must be on her way back to the Atwoods'. She'd hung up. So had Lisa.

And that was how the two girls had come to be glaring at the telephone.

"We can't just wait," said Stevie. "I mean, if she shows up, that's just fine, but if she doesn't and she misses this call from her father, she'll never forgive us for just waiting."

She ran to look out the door. She looked both ways on the street. There was no sign of Carole. She suggested that Lisa call Carole's house. Maybe Carole had been homesick enough to go there. Lisa tried. She got the answering machine.

"Carole, if you're there, pick up the phone," Lisa said. No response. Lisa hung up. It had been worth trying. It just hadn't worked.

"If she's on her way back from Pine Hollow, she could use a lift," Stevie said. "I'll borrow Alex's bike and ride in that direction. I should meet up with her on the way."

"Good idea," said Lisa. "But what's the matter with your bike?"

"Flat tire," Stevie explained.

"Won't Alex mind?" Lisa asked logically.

"He's at soccer practice," said Stevie. "So what he doesn't know . . ."

"Hurry," said Lisa. They were down to twenty-three minutes now.

Alex's bike was lying on the Lakes' front lawn. Stevie picked it up, mounted it, and in a second was on her way toward Pine Hollow. It would be easy to find Carole. There was only one logical route between the stable and the Atwoods' house, so it wasn't as if Carole might choose another way. The route also ran past the shopping center, where Carole might possibly have stopped to pick up something or to look for her friends. Stevie turned into the center's parking lot and rode, illegally, along the sidewalk so that she could look into each of the shops. Carole wasn't in any of them. No sign of her anywhere.

Back on the street, Stevie looked over her shoulder to be sure that Carole hadn't walked by the shopping center while Stevie had been inside. The sidewalk was deserted. No sign of Carole.

And a minute later, there was Pine Hollow. No Carole. Stevie trusted Mrs. Reg and Max to have checked for her, but maybe they'd just checked quickly. She dropped Alex's bike outside the stable, dashed in, yelled, "Carole!" and waited for an answer.

"I told you. She's not here," Max said.

"Just checking," said Stevie.

Without further explanation, she ran out, picked up Alex's bike, and headed back to the Atwoods'. She must have missed Carole. Stevie looked at her watch—fourteen minutes left. With some people, "I'll call you in half an hour" meant that sometime during the afternoon a phone call would come in. With Colonel Hanson, it meant half an hour exactly. Stevie put more pressure on the pedals and kept her eyes peeled. How could she have missed Carole? There weren't that many people who walked around Willow Creek. Surely one, her best friend, would be obvious to Stevie when she saw her.

Stevie still didn't see Carole. She did, however, see

her brother Alex, standing in the middle of the street, forcing her to stop.

"How nice of you to bring me my bike," he said. "You just knew I'd be tired from soccer practice . . ."

"Alex, I—" she began, but she could tell from the look on his face that there was no changing his mind. She relinquished the bike wordlessly and turned her attention to getting back to Lisa's as fast as possible.

She was completely out of breath when she reached the Atwoods' house, and she could hear the phone ringing as she rushed into the foyer.

"Hello?" Lisa said, answering the call.

"Oh, no, she's not here, Colonel Hanson. We've done everything we could to get her here, but she isn't home yet. Well, you could try the stable—" Stevie dashed in and shook her head. "No, don't. Stevie just went over to see if she's there, but she isn't. We don't know where she is. The only thing we're pretty sure of is that she'll be back here in time for dinner at seven-thirty. . . . Oh, you'll be in bed by then?"

Lisa chatted easily with Carole's father. Carole was convinced that he was the best father in the whole wide world, and while Lisa and Stevie both thought their own fathers were great, they had to agree that Colonel Hanson was seriously into the range of Terrific, and they were always glad to talk with him.

Lisa told him that if he couldn't talk to Carole today,

they should decide now when would be a good time, because there probably wasn't anything she could say that would assure Carole that he was okay. "She's really worried about you," Lisa said.

"I don't blame her," Colonel Hanson said. "I'm simply not permitted to say where I am. I can suggest that if she looks at the newspaper, she might get an idea."

"She's been combing through every page of it every morning," Lisa said. "The only international story seems to be that summit meeting in Paris. Carole said this morning that the newspaper reporters are no good at sniffing out the real news."

"Hmmm," said Col. Hanson. "Tell her she shouldn't sell them so short."

"Right, we'll do that. Anyway, you do sound fine, and we'll do our best to convince her that you're okay. Can you call again tomorrow?"

"Same time," he said.

"We'll see that she's here—even if we have to hog-tie her," Lisa promised.

"But we won't have to if she knows you're calling!" Stevie shouted toward the phone.

"Is that my friend Stevie?" the colonel asked. "May I talk to her? I've got a bad joke for her."

"In the flesh," Lisa said, handing the phone to Stevie, who had finally caught her breath. "He's got a bad joke for you."

141

"Hi," Stevie greeted Colonel Hanson. The two of them shared a love of bad jokes, and when either had a new one, he or she had to tell it to the other.

"Do you know what's in the middle of Paris?" he asked.

"Oh, that's easy. It's an old one!" Stevie said. "The answer is *r*."

"Well, there might be another answer this time around. I'll tell you when I get back, okay?"

"Okay," said Stevie, disappointed. She'd been hoping for a new joke to stump her brothers with. On second thought, they were so dense sometimes that she could probably stump them with this one again. "We promise to have Carole here tomorrow," Stevie said.

"Thanks, and bye," Colonel Hanson said, and hung up.

The two girls looked at one another, very sorry that they hadn't been able to get Carole there for the phone call. No matter what else was going on in their lives, Carole's worry about her father was real and serious. They felt as if they'd really let their friend down.

"She's more likely to believe us than she does Sergeant Fowler when we tell her that he sounds just fine," said Lisa.

"But can we really say that?" asked Stevie. "I mean, he sounded just fine, but then he told me that dumb joke!"

"What was so dumb about it?" Lisa asked.

142

"Well, it wasn't really a dumb joke, but he'd told it to me a long time ago. If there's one thing I can count on with the colonel, it's that he never forgets a joke he's told me."

Lisa sat at the kitchen table and began thumbing through the newspapers. She had to find a hint. Colonel Hanson was sure it was there, so it had to be.

"The news should be on TV now," Stevie said. "I'll watch and see if they tell anything, though newspapers usually cover the stories better, and there are more and different—"

"The eyes of the world are focused today on the disarmament talks in Paris," the anchorman said as the TV flicked to life. "Traditional political and military foes have gathered to discuss the elimination of . . ."

Stevie's jaw dropped. Lisa put down the paper and stared at the screen. There, in front of them, from more than three thousand miles away, were hundreds of diplomats and military personnel from all over the world.

"What's in the middle of Paris if it's not an *r*?" asked Stevie.

"Colonel Hanson!" said Lisa. "Whenever they have a conference like this there are always people working secretly in the background. What we see on TV is the staged stuff. You know, the photo ops, the fake handshakes, the big smiles. I bet Colonel Hanson is one of the people doing all the real work behind the scenes!"

It had to be. He was on a secret mission, but it wasn't

in the middle of any desert, and it wasn't in a dangerous land. It was, as he had promised Sergeant Fowler, in a place where he really wanted to take Carole someday. He was in the middle of Paris, France!

"Wait'll we tell Carole!" said Lisa.

"But we've got to find her first," said Stevie.

*Right*, thought Lisa. "Where is she?" she asked, a little annoyed. It was already dark outside, and it was getting late. There was just half an hour until dinner. Was Carole going to do something foolish—like be late again?

THE MINUTE CAROLE and Delilah reached the woods, Carole knew she was doing the right thing. Delilah was tired, but she was definitely invigorated by being outdoors and being in the woods—her favorite place, as well as Carole's.

"Good girl," Carole said, leading Delilah onto a familiar path.

Carole had been riding Starlight almost exclusively since she'd gotten the bay gelding, but before she owned Starlight, she'd ridden every horse at Pine Hollow. Delilah had always been one of her favorites. It felt comfortably familiar to be back in Delilah's saddle now.

Even when she was ill—and Carole couldn't ignore that fact—the mare had a smooth, gentle gait that was in itself soothing. Carole took a deep breath, appreciating the fresh, cool air, tinged with the ever wonderful scent of a horse and its tack. There might also have been a hint of smoke from a burning pile of autumn leaves.

Soon the afternoon sun began to dip behind the hill. Carole looked at her watch. It was getting late. If she'd been at home with her father, they'd be working together to make dinner for themselves. But he wasn't there. He was someplace mysterious and distant. If her father wasn't home, there wasn't any reason to make dinner. She was better off here, with Delilah.

The two of them passed the creek and the rock where Carole so often stopped with her friends. It was one of their favorite places. In warm weather, they could take off their riding boots and dangle their weary feet in the creek. It was shady and quiet; the only sounds were leaves waving in a breeze, an occasional birdsong, and the pleasant sound of the water brushing over rocks in the creek that gave the town its name. Here in the woods, there were no signs of willows, but closer to town, where the creek ran flat through fields, willows had taken root a long time ago.

Carole drew Delilah to a halt and dismounted. She led the mare over to the creek. The water here was high and easy for a horse—or a person—to reach. Delilah sniffed curiously. Her head hung low. She reached forward and took a sip, then stepped back. A sip was all she wanted.

Carole stepped onto one of the rocks in the stream and crouched so that she could fill her hands with water, then lifted them to her lips. It was good and fresh. She wished Delilah would take more. Surely the mare must be thirsty, but she didn't drink any more. She knew what she wanted. Carole accepted that.

She remounted and they went on.

Darkness came quickly now, slipping into the woods and surrounding the travelers. Delilah moved forward on the paths willingly. Carole knew horses had much better night vision than humans, but Delilah's night vision didn't help Carole much.

She looked at her watch again. It was almost eight o'clock. They'd been riding for a couple of hours. She didn't have any idea how far they'd gone or where they were, but she knew Delilah was tired, and so was she. It was time to stop for the night.

Carole had brought some supplies with her. She smiled to herself, realizing that she hadn't had any plan at all when they'd left Pine Hollow, but she had come prepared. Maybe she'd had a plan somewhere in her brain that her brain hadn't told her about.

She dismounted and then removed Delilah's saddle and bridle. The mare seemed to be relieved, and that was good because that was how she was supposed to feel.

Carole snapped a lead rope onto Delilah's halter and then secured the mare to a tree branch, giving her enough rope to reach some fresh greenery that grew on the forest floor and on the few nearby bushes that still had leaves.

For herself, Carole took a granola bar from her backpack. She untied the blanket she'd secured to the back of her saddle and, using the saddle for a pillow, lay down on the ground. She'd seen plenty of cowboys sleep this way in plenty of Western movies. She couldn't think why it wouldn't be a good enough way for her to sleep, too.

It was early for Carole to go to sleep, barely past eight o'clock. But it had been a long, difficult day. She'd been tense and strained until she'd decided to take this trip with Delilah. Now she realized that she was tired. Nearby, she could hear Delilah's even breathing. It soothed her. Soon she slept.

"WHERE IS SHE?" Mrs. Atwood demanded.

Lisa shrugged. "I don't know, Mom."

"I've tried to be nice to her, but this is the second time she's been late to dinner!" Mrs. Atwood said.

"Eleanor," said Mr. Atwood, "it's almost nine o'clock. I don't think this is a case of being late for dinner. I think something's wrong."

"Definitely," Lisa agreed. "You know Carole well enough to know that she isn't the kind of girl who would be that late for dinner. Carole was all upset about her

148

father, and now she's missing. Something is definitely wrong. We've got to find her!"

"Maybe," her mother said. Then she added, "Of course. I'm sorry. I know something has to be wrong. I just didn't want to admit it. It was easier to think she was just late. Okay. Now, where would she have gone?"

"The way I see it, there are two choices," said Lisa. Her parents waited. "The first is Pine Hollow. Max and Mrs. Reg said she wasn't there. So the next choice is her house. Let's call and see if she answers."

Lisa punched in the number. There was no answer. She let the phone ring until the answering machine picked it up. As she had earlier, she spoke into the machine, asking Carole to pick up if she was there. Nobody picked up. She tried again. Still no answer.

"She might just be afraid to answer the phone," said Lisa. "Maybe we should drive out there."

Her father agreed. The two of them drove out to the Hansons' house. The place was completely dark, and there was no sign that anyone had been there. They didn't have a key and couldn't go into the house, but it appeared to be deserted.

They drove back to Lisa's house and reported to Mrs. Atwood.

"Well, according to Lisa, there are only two places she could be. Let's try Pine Hollow again. Maybe she's hiding somewhere there. There are lots of places at the stable where someone could hide, aren't there?"

There were. There were stalls with and without horses; there were lofts, small rooms, basement rooms. The place even had a root cellar, from the days when it had been a working farm.

"Good idea, Mom. Let's call Mrs. Reg."

Mrs. Reg put down the phone with a worried look.

"Max?" she called up the stairs. Max appeared, carrying his daughter, Maxi, who had on a fresh, clean diaper.

"Mrs. Atwood just called. Carole never showed up there this afternoon. Apparently, this is the last place she was seen, and we were the last people to see her. I think we'd better look again. She's been pretty distraught—"

"She's had a lot to be distraught about," Max said.

"Agreed. And she always finds it comforting to be with horses. This is the logical answer. Let's look again. This time, let's look hard."

"I'll be right there," Max said. He took Maxi into Deborah's study, where his wife was working on some research for her latest assignment, and put the baby in the crib next to the desk.

"Carole's missing," he explained to Deborah. "Mother and I have to do a thorough search."

"Oh no, I hope she's okay," said Deborah.

"I'll let you know as soon as we find her," said Max. Then he hurried down the stairs to join his mother in the stable.

It took only a minute to assure themselves that she wasn't in any of the stalls. Starlight looked at them curiously as they passed.

Max checked the tack room; his mother checked her office. Max looked in the feed room; Mrs. Reg checked the locker area.

"Max!" she called out. He joined her there. "Here's her book bag and her school shoes," she said. "She must have brought her riding clothes and changed into them."

"But her horse is here," Max protested. "I triple-checked Starlight's stall."

"And I double-checked it, but neither of us has checked Delilah's stall, have we?"

"Delilah's not here now," Max said. "She's over in the— Oh, my! Let's go."

He grabbed a flashlight from the shelf in his mother's office, and the two of them hurried over to the feed shed. This had to be the answer, and they both knew it.

The door of the shed was open. Delilah's stall was empty.

Mrs. Reg and Max stepped outside and looked at the

woods that lay beyond the fields. "Oh no!" said Mrs. Reg, shaking her head with concern.

Max tugged at his mother's sleeve. "We've got some phone calls to make," he said, steering her back to the office.

"And no time to waste," agreed Mrs. Reg.

CAROLE FELT SOMETHING brushing her cheek. She swatted at it. It was still there. She swatted again. Still there. Reluctantly she opened her eyes.

That something was an oak leaf. Carole shook her head, trying to clear her thoughts. It took a second, but then she realized that she was in the woods. She'd been sleeping on the ground, which began to explain how uncomfortable she'd been, and it was a cool, gray morning. The coolness suggested a reason for her dreams about the North Pole a full two months before Christmas!

"Oh," she said, finally remembering why she was in the woods. There, to her left, was Delilah, resting quietly. Carole and Delilah were on a trail ride—a

153

long trail ride, but a trail ride. They'd gone to sleep when it became dark, and now that it was becoming light, they were waking up, or at least Carole was. She looked at her watch. It was six-thirty. The sun was up, a little bit. It was another day, and Delilah was still alive.

Carole stood up and brushed herself off. Breaking camp was a pretty simple matter. All she had to eat was another granola bar. There was grass for Delilah if she wanted any, but she didn't seem to. A few minutes after waking, Carole had Delilah tacked up, and the two of them were off for another day of riding.

Carole had done a lot of trail riding in her life. She'd ridden trails wherever she'd lived before she moved to Willow Creek; she'd ridden trails out West when she and her friends visited Kate Devine at the Bar None Ranch. She'd ridden in the Rockies; she'd ridden in the Appalachians; she'd ridden through snowdrifts in Minnesota. And she'd been riding the trails near Pine Hollow ever since her family had moved to Willow Creek. She'd always known where she was headed and how she was going to get there, though she hadn't always gone the right way.

This was another trail ride. It had to be because she and Delilah were on a trail. The big difference was that Carole didn't have any idea what trail they were on or where it headed. She knew that the woods behind Pine Hollow went on for miles. Some of it was state forest.

154

Some of it was private land. All of it had trails, but none of it was well marked. They were completely lost. And it was okay.

"Come on, girl, let's get going," Carole said, knowing it didn't matter where they went, just that they were going. Delilah picked up her pace to a slow walk, and they continued on their way.

"ALL RIGHT NOW, groups of three," Max was saying to all the people who stood around him in a circle. Next to him was a policeman. He was handing out maps to one person in each group.

"Each of these maps is marked with a sector. You should be looking on and around the trails in that sector only. If you leave your sector, you'll be doubling somebody else's efforts."

"Where do we go?" Lisa asked, reaching for a map.

"Back home!" ordered the policeman. "We don't want any kids joining in the search for this girl, or the next thing we know, we'll be looking for three girls, not two." He turned his back on Lisa and Stevie.

The girls glared at him. "Like he knows as much about Carole or the woods as we do," Stevie said.

Lisa rolled her eyes.

The policeman also gave each group a flare and a noisemaker so that anyone who found Carole and Delilah could signal all the other searchers.

It wasn't even seven o'clock in the morning, but there

155

were loads of people at Pine Hollow. Max and his mother had spent a good deal of the evening before marshaling neighbors and stable riders to find Carole. Everybody knew Carole. Everybody knew Delilah. And everybody cared about both of them. Since the Pine Hollow horses were quarantined, all the searching was to be done on foot. A few people who did not keep their horses at Pine Hollow had them trailered nearby so that they could ride into the woods on them.

"Okay, off you go!" said the policeman. As if it were the beginning of a race, a hundred people ran across the field and headed into Pine Hollow's woods. Max was among them. Mrs. Reg showed the policemen to her office, where they could set up a command center. A number of people had radios with them, and quite a few also carried cellular telephones. All information was to come to Mrs. Reg's office.

As soon as the area was clear, Stevie and Lisa looked at one another. The policeman might have thought that they belonged at home, but they knew better. Their job was to look for Carole. Also, they knew it was against the rules, but sometimes there were things that were more important than rules. They were going to ride, and nothing and nobody would stop them.

The girls surreptitiously tacked up Belle and Starlight, paused to touch the good-luck horseshoe, and were half-way across the field before anybody noticed.

The policeman called after them to stop. Then they heard Mrs. Reg talking to him.

"You could no more keep those two girls from riding after their friend than you could hold back the tide. Now, come back into the office where you can do some good!"

Lisa and Stevie looked at one another and laughed.

"Mrs. Reg has a lot of common sense," said Stevie.

"A lot more than that policeman, anyway," Lisa agreed. She leaned forward and whispered into Starlight's ear. "Find Carole!" she said. She could have sworn that Starlight lengthened his stride as soon as he heard her words.

DELILAH'S PACE SLOWED. She was doing all she could to satisfy her rider's request, but her best wasn't very fast now.

"Want to stop, girl?" Carole asked.

Delilah's answer was to take a deep breath and push forward. A lifetime of doing what she was asked by her riders made her willing to move ahead, blindly doing exactly what she was asked.

"You don't know any other way but the right way, do you, Delilah?" Carole asked.

Delilah let out her breath. It sounded like a sigh. Carole held the reins ever so slightly closer to her own hips.

Delilah responded to that subtle signal as she always had. She stopped.

Carole climbed down out of the saddle. She stepped around and looked at the mare. The signs were unmistakable now. The symptoms that had been slight the day before were now readily apparent. Carole was even more certain: Delilah had EIA, and she was dying.

Carole reached up and patted the mare's neck. Delilah looked at her, her eyes filled with trust. She'd always been treated well by people. This was not a time when she was going to stop trusting humans. Carole was touched by Delilah's willingness. She also understood, or was pretty sure she understood, that she was doing the right thing for this horse.

This mare—always a faithful stable horse, a fine, caring mother, and a good, obedient school horse—was not one to give up and die in a stall. She deserved to be in the woods, her favorite place, and she deserved to be with someone she trusted—Carole. Sure this was a slightly irrational thing for Carole to be doing with Delilah, but if Delilah was going to die, she should be able to die in a place that made her happy, and she should be able to be with someone she liked and who loved her.

"Don't worry, Delilah," Carole said softly. "I'm here with you, forever."

The only thing she didn't know was how long forever would be.

\* \* \*

158

"CAROLE! CAROLE! ARE you there?" Lisa called out into the thick woods.

There was no answer. She hadn't thought there would be. Carole had been gone almost fifteen hours. She and Stevie had been on the trail for only one hour. Surely Carole had gotten farther than this!

"We'll find her. She'll hear us and she'll call out to us," Stevie said. "In the meantime, what we can do is ride and talk so that she can hear us."

"You don't think she'll be hiding?" Lisa asked.

"Not from us," Stevie said. Lisa knew Stevie was right.

"Okay," Lisa agreed. "I guess that for now, the most important thing to do is to cover land so we can catch up with her—wherever she is."

"Right. This way, then," said Stevie, pointing left when they came to the first fork in the trail.

"Why that way?" Lisa asked.

"I have no idea," said Stevie.

Together they turned left.

CAROLE LOOKED UP at the sky. It seemed a little threatening. Then she realized it wasn't threatening rain. It was threatening evening. Was it possible that she and Delilah had been riding all day long? She looked at her watch. It was six o'clock already. They'd been going for eleven hours, ever since they'd left their camp. She'd ridden some of the day and walked some of the day.

Delilah, ever willing to do what was asked of her, kept on going, moving as she was told, with or without a rider on her back.

Carole had never seen anything like the courage the mare was showing. With every step, she became more convinced that she was doing what was right for Delilah. Otherwise, why would the mare keep going? This wasn't a horse that would be satisfied to wait for death.

Well, it was getting dark now. Carole was both tired and hungry. It was time to find someplace that might offer shelter for her and for Delilah for the night.

She signaled Delilah to stop. She took her feet out of the stirrups and allowed them to hang loosely. It helped relax her. She looked around. The woods seemed slightly familiar, but that didn't seem possible. They'd been moving for hours and hours, and unless they'd been making a gigantic circle, they had to be at least twenty miles from Pine Hollow.

Carole looked around her again. She knew so much of the forest in the area, but a lot of unfamiliar forest could seem familiar because it was similar. The trees were the same kinds that grew right next to Pine Hollow. The rocks were the same sort that filled those woods. It was comforting to be so far from home but so close to the familiar.

There was a rustle in the underground. Carole looked. It was a squirrel. He was running very fast. Carole wondered what he was running from, and then her question was answered. She heard the sharp bark of a coyote, then saw it dash across the trail. It startled her.

It startled Delilah even more. Without warning, Delilah took off. Carole was unprepared to have this ill horse bolt from under her. She grabbed the reins tightly and then tried to regain the stirrups with her feet, but that only made her legs flail wildly and threatened to unbalance and unseat her completely. Carole gripped with her legs and grabbed the palomino's mane as tightly as she could.

It wasn't enough. As the coyote disappeared, chasing the squirrel, Delilah veered downhill, off the path—and right toward a tree!

The mare shifted to the left of the tree, but Carole could tell this was going to be bad news for her. A horse, even a sick one, would always make room for itself to pass by an obstacle like a tree, but there was no guarantee that there would be room for the rider's legs to clear it, especially when they were flapping without the aid of stirrups. She could be bruised, crushed, or pushed off the horse. Carole had no choice. She let herself fall off Delilah two feet before she would have been scraped off by the tree.

When she landed, her hip hit a rock or a root, she didn't know or care which. She knew it hurt a lot and was going to leave her with a big swelling and, eventually, a gigantic bruise.

She sat up and looked to see what had happened to

Delilah. It wasn't much. The horse had made it past the tree that had frightened Carole, but a large boulder sat right in front of her. She could have run around it. She could have run left or right. There was plenty of room, but as soon as she'd gotten to the boulder, she'd stopped. On another day, Carole might have thought that Delilah had stopped because she was embarrassed to have thrown Carole. Today, however, Carole was pretty sure that Delilah had stopped because bolting and running had taken all her energy. From where she sat on the ground, Carole could see Delilah's sides heaving in and out, gasping for air from the very brief sprint. *It's time to stop running*, Carole thought. *It's time to rest.*

"Okay, Delilah," she said, pulling herself slowly to a standing position. "This is where we're going to camp for the night."

Delilah didn't even turn around to look at her.

"WHAT DO YOU mean, you're going to get a C in history!" Stevie couldn't believe her ears.

"That's right," said Lisa. "I can get whatever grade I want to get, and just think what it'll show people if I get a C."

"Well, it'll show them you're nuts, for starters," Stevie said. She wasn't very good at holding her tongue. She hoped she wouldn't regret what she'd just said, but she didn't care if she regretted it. She meant it.

"No, I don't think so," said Lisa. "It'll show people that I'm not obsessive about my grades. I can get As all right. Everybody knows that. What they don't know is that I can let go a bit and get a C."

"You're going to have to work very hard to get a C," said Stevie.

"I know," Lisa told her. "But I can do it. I just know I can."

Stevie was glad Lisa was in the lead, because that meant Lisa couldn't see her face and the contortions it was going through. This decision was even crazier than Lisa's determination to get an A+ and the fact that she was working on a paper six months early.

Stevie needed help. No, actually, it was Lisa who needed help, but Stevie knew that she, Stevie, was going to need help in order to help Lisa. When were they going to find Carole?

"It's getting dark," said Lisa. "What do you want to do?"

"Camp, I guess," said Stevie, pulling Belle up next to Lisa and Starlight.

"You brought a sleeping bag?" Lisa asked.

"Sure, and we can share. And I brought some stuff to eat, but I don't think it's very good. Just some candy."

"It'll go perfectly with the fruit and yogurt I brought along. And we don't have to share the sleeping bag. I brought mine, too," Lisa said, pointing to the bundle on the rear of her saddle.

"Two great minds with a single thought," Stevie said. It was nice to know that even while she was worried about finding Carole, Lisa was right there and totally prepared to help her with Carole's problem.

"Here, this looks like a nice enough place," Stevie said, climbing down out of Belle's saddle. Lisa dismounted as well.

"It does look like a nice place. In fact, it looks like such a nice place that I think somebody else found it before we did."

The two girls looked around them. They had to look hard in the fading light, but it was clear that someone had been there very recently. There was an area where the ground had been flattened in a manner that looked suspiciously like a sleeping body. The tree nearby had a branch hanging down that was perfect for tying a lead rope.

"Look at this!" Lisa said. Stevie's eyes followed Lisa's finger. There, on the branch, was a small knot of hair. It was long hair. It was silver.

"Delilah's mane?" Stevie asked.

"Either that or a long-haired old lady got tied to the tree."

"We're definitely on their trail, then," Stevie said, excited.

"Sure, but a day late, I think," Lisa said. "That's good news, bad news."

"Well, at least it's the right direction," Stevie reminded her friend.

"There's that," Lisa agreed.

The girls cooled down their horses by walking them gently for a few minutes. Then they found some grass and leaves for them to eat—though they were careful to keep Belle away from the kind of grass that she was allergic to—and they found a rill that they presumed would eventually lead downhill to Willow Creek.

It had been a very long day for the two of them, and they'd hardly slept the night before because they'd been so worried. They hadn't wanted anybody to worry about them, but they knew Mrs. Reg knew where they were. Mrs. Reg also had excellent vision and would have seen that they each had a sleeping bag. Nobody would seriously worry about them, except maybe Lisa's mother, but Mrs. Reg would calm her quickly.

They shared some of the food they'd brought along, saving enough for breakfast, and then laid out their sleeping bags. The sun was fully down now. They couldn't see much, and they couldn't light a fire. There was really only one thing to do, so they did it. They slept.

CAROLE OPENED HER eyes. It was still dark, but something had awakened her. When she and Delilah had stopped for the night, they had been on a gentle slope, next to a very big rock—a boulder, really. It had split at some point, and a small chunk of it had fallen down next to the larger, main piece, making something like a tent-shaped cave. Carole had secured Delilah to a tree branch as she had the night before and then settled in under the cover of the cave in the rock. She'd been exhausted and had slept soundly, but now something woke her up.

She stepped out from under the rock and looked around. Her eyes were completely adjusted to the dark of the woods. The moon shone overhead, and small bits of moonlight made splatters on the ground nearby. There was something else light on the ground, too, and then Carole knew what had awakened her. It had been Delilah, lowering herself to the ground for a rest.

Some horses sleep lying down, some standing up. Delilah was a standing horse. Carole thought the only time she'd ever seen Delilah lying down was when she was giving birth to Samson. It was unlike her, but then, so was being sick.

Carole picked up her blanket and went over to Delilah. The mare was shivering. It wasn't cold that night, not even as cool as the night before. Delilah's fever was up, though. Carole knew it just by touching her. She put her blanket over the mare, who blinked once in acknowledgment, perhaps thanks. Carole got down on the ground next to her, lying against the mare's back and resting her head across her neck. Delilah's soft mane was all the pillow Carole needed.

Carole's blanket wasn't large enough to warm Delilah, but the proximity of her own body would help soothe the ailing mare. Delilah breathed in deeply and exhaled slowly. Carole saw her eyes close. They both slept again.

* * *

STEVIE AWOKE WITH a start. Nearby, something had rustled—the wind, a squirrel, she didn't know what. It didn't frighten her. She'd slept in the woods enough to know there was nothing to be afraid of.

She sat up and looked around. Suddenly a feeling of familiarity swept over her. It took a moment to recognize where the feeling had come from, and then she remembered. It was from the book she'd been reading. She was actually sleeping in the same woods, perhaps on the same ground, that Hallie had slept on when she'd made her run on the Underground Railroad. Had she sipped water from the same rill where Stevie and Lisa had washed their faces the night before? Had she seen the same sky, the same stars and moon, whose light now filtered through the branches overhead? Had she heard the same rustling?

The story that had felt so real as she had read it felt even more real as she realized that she was sort of living it. A lot of people traveled on paths to freedom. Some of the paths were on the Underground Railroad; some paths took a horse somewhere to die in peace; some paths led straight to Cs. The trouble was that sometimes these paths were dreams come true, like Hallie's path to Canada, and sometimes they were nightmares. Stevie hoped her friends would find their dreams and not their nightmares!

Stevie rolled over then and went back to sleep, dreaming of moonlight and successful journeys.

21

IN THE END, it was easy for Lisa and Stevie to find Carole. They knew they had started on the right path as soon as they woke up. What they didn't know was that Delilah was so sick and so weak that she and Carole had hardly made any progress at all the day before.

Every time Lisa and Stevie found strands of Delilah's silky mane and tail along the path, they knew they were getting closer. They called softly as they proceeded, only unsure how soon they would find their friend.

"Carole!"

"It's Lisa and Stevie, Carole, are you there?"

"We've got Belle and Starlight with us!"

"Carole?"

By noon their voices were tired, but their horses were

not. The girls proceeded slowly, carefully, calling less often and finding more signs of their friend's presence. Here a swatch of silvery hair, there a small manure dropping. Then they found a granola bar wrapper.

"Carole?" Lisa called out softly. In the distance, she could hear the gentle trickle of a small brook. It made sense that Carole would be near water.

There was a sound. Was it a response?

"Carole?" Stevie called a little more loudly.

"Stevie?" came a hushed cry. "Lisa? I'm here. Come on over. But don't bring the horses."

"She's there!" Lisa said to Stevie. "It's Carole!"

Stevie and Lisa both knew they'd come to their journey's end. Carole was somewhere in the woods, off to the right of the trail.

And Carole didn't want them to bring their horses. Certainly Carole would know that they'd come on horseback to find her. But she would want to protect the horses. That confirmed what both of them already suspected. Delilah was sick with EIA. They couldn't risk exposing Belle and Starlight to the disease.

"We'll be there in a minute," Stevie assured their friend. The girls dismounted and walked the horses back down the trail a few hundred feet. At this time of year, with the weather so cool, there was little chance of a tabanid's being handy to carry any disease from one horse to another, but none of the three girls was interested in taking any risk. Stevie and Lisa secured the two horses to low-slung branches and took off into the woods toward the place where they'd heard Carole's cry.

As soon as they saw Carole, they understood everything. Their friend was sitting on the ground, next to Delilah. The mare was lying limply, her head weakly resting on Carole's knees. She was dying.

Carole rubbed the mare's face softly in the way Delilah always liked best. Stevie sat down across the horse from Carole and began stroking her soft neck. Lisa sat next to Carole by the mare's back and patted her withers.

Delilah took in a slow, difficult breath. The girls held their own and kept on patting. The mare breathed out. The girls sighed.

"It's okay, Delilah," Carole said. "You've been wonderful to us. You don't have to thank us. Each of us has ridden you and loved you as long as we've known you. We need to thank you for all you've done for us."

"We've been through a lot together," Stevie said. "Remember when Samson was born? What a champion you were. You had the three most ignorant midwives in Virginia looking after you, and you didn't let us down at all. You made us look good!"

"Best of all, you brought us Samson," said Lisa. "That beautiful little colt. You can be proud of him, Delilah. People always think of Cobalt when they think of Samson, but the fact is that he's got your fine character, your kindness, your stamina and willingness. Max says he'll make a wonderful school horse one of these days. Personally, I think he's championship material."

"Just like his mother," Carole added. "You never took a wrong step with me. No matter how hard I worked you, you always worked harder, teaching me with every step you took. That goes for the last few years, as long as I've known you, but it also goes for the last few days. No matter what, you were determined to please me. What a horse."

"What a champion," said Stevie.

"What a friend," said Lisa.

The girls held the mare and patted her. Stevie reached to her belly and put her hand on the horse's heart. They watched her breathing slow, and they waited. They didn't talk. There was nothing more to say.

Delilah's breathing grew more rapid and shallower. Her eyes stayed closed. Then the breaths became irregular. And then they stopped.

"Her heart's stopped," Stevie told her friends. They nodded.

Delilah's journey was over.

"Dear God," Stevie said, speaking softly, "take her and give her a home in horse heaven."

"With Cobalt," Carole added.

The girls reached to each other across Delilah and took one another's hands, joining in a circle. And then they sobbed.

"Girls? stevie? carole? lisa?"

"Max?" Carole asked.

"I guess," said Lisa. "Someone was bound to find us. There must be a zillion searchers out here."

"Looking for me?" Carole wondered.

"Worried about you," Stevie said. "When you disappeared and a horse was missing from Pine Hollow, well, people were worried. There were police and a lot of people going through these woods, with maps, flares, and noisemakers, all looking for you."

"Over here!" Lisa called.

Max found them and then ran over to Delilah. He nodded, understanding.

"Judy called us last night and told us her test was

positive," Max said. "But we knew it already. She was showing all the symptoms."

"You knew?" Carole was surprised that they hadn't said anything.

"We didn't want anyone to panic. We also didn't think it would be this fast, but it was this fast with King Perry, too, so it appears to be a particularly virulent form of the disease. You girls were smart to park the horses down the path."

"Carole told us to," Lisa said.

"But we would have done it anyway," Stevie added.

"When did she die?" Max asked, patting the mare softly.

"Just a few minutes ago," Carole told him. "We were all with her. We took care of her. She wasn't in pain. It was just like she was too tired to live."

"That's the way this disease goes," said Max. "It's a horrible disease. I hope and pray that all the other horses in the stable are all right."

"Their tests were negative, weren't they?" Carole asked.

"Oh, sure. And there's really no reason to believe that they'll be anything but negative. Delilah had just returned from Hedgerow. We know where she contracted swamp fever, and considering the fact that the weather's been cool since her return—not a good season for tabanid—we don't expect any of the other horses to get it. But we'll take every precaution to see that they don't.

174

"Anyway, although I can't applaud your extended trail ride, Carole, I'm glad you were with Delilah and that you stuck with her to the end. You three have been a good friend to her."

"She's been a good friend to us," Lisa told him.

"That, too," Max agreed. "Now, let's set everybody's mind at ease as to your whereabouts, Carole, and then head back to Pine Hollow."

The return. Carole hadn't even thought about that. It had taken her two days on an ailing horse to get where she was. How long would it take them all to get back? She asked Max the question.

"About half an hour, I think," he said.

"So fast?" Stevie asked.

"Well, we're only about two miles away."

Carole almost laughed. She'd ridden almost twenty hours and she'd only gone two miles!

"All the trails around here crisscross," he said. "You could probably go fifty miles and never backtrack. It's just a matter of knowing where you are."

He stood up and helped Carole, Lisa, and Stevie stand up, too. Carole felt a little stiff. She'd been sitting there on the ground with Delilah for a long time. She stretched and shook out her arms and legs.

Stevie looked at Delilah and then at her friend. What Carole had done was foolish, of course, but it was courageous, too. It took the same kind of courage that—

Something caught Stevie's eye. It was the very large

boulder behind Carole. There it was, set on a hillside, a small creek nearby. A chunk of the boulder had somehow been broken off the larger piece and had fallen to the earth, leaning against the larger boulder, making a small tentlike structure, almost a cave. And there, above the tent on the main boulder, was a large, unmistakable arrow. Stevie could hardly believe her eyes.

"Oh, isn't that neat?" Carole asked when she noticed what Stevie was staring at. "I slept in there last night. It seemed very cozy. I only came out when it was clear that Delilah was getting sicker."

"Right," Stevie said, but she wasn't thinking about how cozy it must have been for Carole. She was thinking about how terrifying it must have been for someone else—Hallie! Stevie knew she was right. There wasn't an ounce of doubt in her mind. She'd found Hallie's hiding place! Hallie was real. Hallie *had* traveled on the Underground Railroad right through Willow Creek and Pine Hollow.

She gulped. Should she tell? Well, neither of her friends had read the book yet. It wouldn't really mean anything until they had. She'd wait. It would be her surprise—well, hers and one other person's. As soon as she got home, she was going to write a letter to Elizabeth Wallingford Johnson. She couldn't wait.

"I guess I'm ready to go now," Carole told Max and her friends. She picked up her granola bar wrapper. She didn't want to leave anything behind. She looked at

Delilah, who still had the blanket covering her. It seemed right and decent to leave it there.

"I'll follow you girls," Max said. "I just need to say good-bye to an old friend first."

They understood completely.

# 23

"WHO'S THAT?" CAROLE asked, looking over Lisa's shoulder at the crowd of people who stood outside the stable at Pine Hollow.

"Those are your searchers," Stevie said. "It's everybody who was worried enough about you to tromp through the woods yesterday and today."

"I think they were also looking for *us* today," Stevie said.

"Oh, right. I forgot that we broke the rules," Lisa said.

"It's good for you to break the rules every once in a while," Carole teased her.

"I'm trying," Lisa said.

Suddenly someone in the group spotted the girls

emerging from the woods. Several people started waving. Then everyone was waving—and cheering.

"Aren't they angry with us?" Stevie asked. She knew people would be relieved to find out they were all right, but surely somebody was going to be annoyed.

"Probably not," said Lisa. "Max had a cellular telephone with him. As we were riding off, he was calling Pine Hollow to say we were fine. I'll bet you he told everyone we'd done something heroic and should be welcomed."

"It didn't seem very heroic to me," Carole said. "Just logical."

"Well, it seemed heroic to him," Lisa said. "Remember, Max cares about his horses as much as we do."

That was true. Max had never been as worried about Carole as other people because he'd always understood exactly what she was doing—just as Mrs. Reg had, which was why she had pooh-poohed the policeman who'd tried to stop Lisa and Stevie.

They had a lot of confidence in The Saddle Club. They were sure the girls knew what they were doing with horses, and they knew the girls could take care of themselves when they camped in the woods. In short, they'd been more worried about Delilah than about Carole or her friends. And they'd been right to be. Carole felt a certain warmth from knowing that. Max and Mrs. Reg really trusted them.

The girls waved back at the welcoming crowd. Starlight and Belle picked up a trot. It was time to get home.

A few minutes later, the girls were close enough to distinguish faces in the crowd. Since it was a Sunday and nobody had to be at school or work, the whole place was filled with welcoming faces.

"I see your parents, Stevie," Carole said. "They're smiling."

"What about mine?" Lisa asked nervously.

"There they are," Carole said. "They're smiling, too. And standing next to them is . . . is . . . is . . ."

Could it be true? Carole squinted to be sure she was seeing right. After all, she hadn't seen him in a while— maybe five days. He could have changed. No, her eyes weren't fooling her. It definitely was true.

"Dad!" she called out.

Starlight broke into a canter. He knew when it was time to go fast!

The next fifteen minutes were a blur of questions, hugs, and tears. The police took complete notes, and then, satisfied that everybody was happy and healthy, they closed up their command center and left the denizens of Pine Hollow to their reunion. All the other people who'd joined in the hunt for the girls hugged them, welcomed them, told them how relieved they were to know they were all right, and left them alone with their families and the Regnerys.

180

"Are you home for good?" Carole asked her father after she'd given him his umpteenth hug.

"No, honey, I've got to go back, but everybody is taking the weekend off, so I am, too. I just traveled a little farther than the rest of the group."

"Where were you, Dad? Can you tell me now?"

"I can, but it has to be a secret between you and me. You can't tell anyone, including your best friends. When I'm back for good, then we can talk about it, and I should be able to tell you some things, but for now—"

"Colonel Hanson?" Stevie said, interrupting the father-daughter reunion.

"Yes, Stevie," he said.

"I figured out the new answer to the old joke you told me," she said.

"And it is?" he asked.

"You," she said.

He smiled and put his finger to his lips. "Can't tell anyone that joke for a while," he said.

"I promise," she said. "National security and all."

Then he leaned over to his daughter and whispered in her ear.

"Really?" she said. "And I thought you wanted to take me to a desert!"

He laughed then, long and loud. Carole thought it was the sweetest sound she'd ever heard!

"So what are you doing here?" Carole asked. "I mean, how did you get allowed to come all the way home?"

"It was after I spoke with Lisa and Stevie the other day. They kept telling me that you were doing just fine, no problems, there was nothing for me to worry about. I didn't believe them for a minute. They were worried about you, but they didn't want me to be. So I just had to get home. I couldn't leave before last night, but here I am. And I'm all yours until Monday morning, when my transport takes off to deliver me back to, um, my destination. It isn't long, but we'll both stay at the Atwoods', because our house is all locked up. And we'll have the rest of today together. Want to go on a picnic or something?"

"Actually, Dad, I think I've had enough of the great outdoors for a little while."

"How about going back to Lisa's house and having a nice hot bath?"

"Now you're talking," she said, and hugged him one more time.

"I'm ready for a shower, too," Stevie said to her parents. "Can we go now?"

"Sure," they agreed. Stevie did want to take a shower, but even before she did that, she had a letter to write with some really exciting news for one Elizabeth Wallingford Johnson.

# 24

"OUCH!" CAROLE SAID, settling onto the top of one of Pine Hollow's fences.

"Is that still bothering you?" Lisa asked, perching next to her.

Carole nodded.

"It's already been four weeks since Delilah threw you and you landed on those rocks and roots in the woods," Stevie said, joining her friends. The three of them had been riding in Pine Hollow's schooling ring after their Pony Club meeting and now decided to watch Max give a lesson while they chatted. Their horses were secured nearby, waiting to be groomed.

"Think of it more like, 'It's *only* been four weeks,' " Carole said. "When I landed on the forest floor, I landed hard. Those are deep bruises, about which I can do nothing."

"Except complain," Stevie teased.

"I have to take my pleasures where I can find them," Carole said, teasing back.

"So these days, her main pleasures are reading the newspaper and complaining," Lisa put in.

"I'm starting to love the newspaper," Carole agreed. "Every day I can read more about a certain top secret disarmament conference in a certain top secret location, and while it's not exactly like getting a letter or talking to him every day, it's nearly as good, especially now that the newspaper has started using phrases like *winding down*. I know Dad will be home soon."

"And in the meantime," said Stevie, "he's spending every evening and weekend scoping out neat places to take you when you go with him to a certain top secret location, right?"

"*Absolument,*" Carole agreed in her best French.

"Well, there's other good news around here," Lisa said. "All the horses still seem to be healthy."

"That is good news," Carole agreed. "But we're really not going to know for sure until the full forty-five days have passed. That's another two weeks. They could be a long two weeks. Also, it's possible for horses to carry the virus for a long time without showing any symptoms at all. That's why they have to be tested frequently."

"Sure, but nobody really believes any of the other horses got infected, do they?" Lisa asked.

"Nobody really knows," said Carole. "And that's the truth." It was a scary truth, but all three girls knew they had to accept it.

"Well, in the meantime, all the horses seem to be totally healthy," Stevie said, bringing a slightly cheerier note to the conversation.

"That is, if you don't count three sore legs on Barq, Nero, and Nickel, and a case of colic that I diagnosed in Patch last week," Carole said, more than a little proud of her latest diagnostic coup.

"You're really doing a wonderful job here, Carole," Stevie said. "Your sharp eyes have saved two horses from having minor colic turn into major colic by spotting it early. Max must be showering you with compliments."

"Right," Carole agreed. "He said, 'Nice work, Carole.' "

"Wow!" said Lisa. "Max really went overboard with that!" She was joking, but they all knew that Max gave compliments sparingly. He expected his students to do well, and he didn't remark when they merely did well. "Nice work" was a big compliment from him.

"Hmmm," Stevie said. "Seems to me it wasn't all that long ago that you were furious because your history teacher—Mr. Mathios?—said you'd done nice work. Have you changed your mind about what constitutes a compliment?"

185

She said it in a cheerful voice, but both she and Carole were a little nervous about what Lisa's response would be. They hadn't talked with Lisa about her history class and her competitive tendencies when it came to grades since Lisa's announcement that she was going to get a C. They both considered that plan so un-Lisa-like that there hardly seemed anything at all they could say about it.

Lisa was oblivious to their concern. "Oh, Mr. Mathios definitely trained at the same school of compliments as Max did! The other day, I did a presentation on Woodrow Wilson's Fourteen Points, explaining them to the class. When I was done, he said 'Very interesting,' but when I got the report back, he'd given me an A-plus."

"Not a C?" Carole asked hesitantly.

"No way!" said Lisa. "I did really great work. Why would he have given me a C?"

"Um, Lisa," Stevie began, "you told us you were going to prove that grades weren't important by getting a C in that class."

"I almost forgot," Lisa said. "It seems so long ago that I thought that. But it was a dumb idea from the beginning, and the only mystery is why you two didn't tell me so. See, I'd gotten all hung up about Fiona Jamieson, and she's not what's important to me. *I'm* what's important to me. If I need to get a good grade to feel good about myself, I have to work to get a good grade. I certainly don't have to work to beat Fiona, and besides, it doesn't matter anymore."

"Why's that?" Carole asked.

"Something happened to Fiona. I don't know what it was. But right about then, when Delilah died and you ran away and I was going nuts about getting a C, Fiona sort of fell apart, like she'd burned out or something. I have no idea what happened, but she's been out of school as much as she's been in since then, and her grades have really dropped. Not that anyone tells us who got which grade, but you sort of know. I feel sorry for her. I wish I could help."

Carole thought back to the day she'd met Fiona in the library. She remembered how angry she'd gotten at the girl, wondering if she had really been angry at Fiona, or at Lisa for being so foolish about a history class, or at herself for being so confused. Whomever she had been angry at, it was Fiona who had taken the brunt of it, and then, right after that, she'd fallen apart. Carole had never told her friends about her run-in with Fiona. She did now. She asked Lisa if she thought she might have hurt Fiona. She hadn't meant to hurt her. She'd just needed to be honest.

"Whatever caused Fiona's problems wasn't you," Lisa said. "She's been like she is for a long time. I know these feelings build up and then they sort of spill over. It's happened to me, but I've been luckier than Fiona. I've had friends like you to help me when I start heading for trouble. Fiona doesn't have any close friends. So, no, Carole, it's not your fault. I promise."

Stevie reassured Carole, too, but she wasn't quite as gentle as Lisa had been. "Look, anybody who's pulling down an A-plus in a class and is trying to get extra credit is already nuts. You didn't do anything that would make her more nuts, because how much more nuts could you get than that?"

Stevie kept thinking about Fiona, but not in the same way that Lisa and Carole were thinking about her. It occurred to Stevie that if Fiona was no longer going to be a local history genius, then there was an opening for the next prodigy, and she was available for the job. Wouldn't that surprise her friends! The same night that The Saddle Club had returned from the woods, Stevie had written to Elizabeth Wallingford Johnson about the discovery of Hallie's hiding place. She was a little surprised that she hadn't heard from the author yet, but she'd sent the letter to the publisher of the book, who would forward it to her, and that probably took a while. And, because she'd written such a wonderful book, Elizabeth Wallingford Johnson probably got a lot of mail and couldn't answer it all at once. But as soon as she saw Stevie's letter, she was sure to write or call. What a discovery Stevie had made! There, in the middle of the woods of Virginia, she'd found the exact rock that Hallie had described in her diary. There was no doubt about it. It formed a cave and it had the arrow shape chipped out of it. Carole and Delilah had camped at exactly the same place where Hallie and Esther had camped so many years before.

"That was a great Horse Wise meeting," Carole said.

"I'll like it better when we can have mounted meetings again," said Lisa.

Since nobody was allowed to bring any horses or ponies to Pine Hollow until the quarantine was lifted, they were only having unmounted meetings, because a lot of the members brought their own ponies to mounted meetings. It meant they were learning an awful lot, but it also meant that they couldn't ride as a group or play games or practice skills on their own horses. It wasn't surprising, then, that the girls had taken the time, after the meeting, to do some work together in the schooling ring.

"I would have preferred to go on a trail ride," Stevie said.

"Well, we'll be able to do that pretty soon," Lisa said. "Like as soon as all the horses pass their next blood test, right?"

"There's a little matter of getting Max's permission, too," Carole reminded her. "Although he was slightly glad we were all with Delilah, he was not exactly thrilled about the police and the hundreds of people who went to look for all of us, and I definitely heard him mumble something about how we'd used up ten years' worth of trail rides in those two days."

"Oh, don't worry," Stevie said. "We'll talk him out of it."

"How?" Lisa asked, genuinely curious.

"Somehow," Stevie said. That was a word that tended to frighten her friends. If she didn't have anything in mind, she was likely to jump on the first wild scheme that popped into her head, and those were always trouble—even when they were fun.

Behind them Starlight gave a gentle whinny.

"He thinks we're ignoring him," Carole said, looking over her shoulder at her beloved horse.

"Well, he's right," Lisa said. "It's time to pay attention to our horses and take care of them the way they want to be taken care of."

"You mean spoil them rotten?" Stevie asked.

"That's what they have in mind," Lisa said.

"Sounds good to me," Carole added.

The girls climbed down from the fence and set to work. It was a wonderfully ordinary set of tasks they had to do, and the girls knew they would enjoy every bit of it. Caring for horses was so necessary and so compelling that it was impossible to fret or worry about anything else—especially now that there seemed to be so little to fret about anyway.

Carole was almost as certain as her friends that all the

Pine Hollow horses would be found free of the EIA virus. She now knew where her father was, that he wasn't in any danger at all (except for eating too much French food!), and she had a good idea that he'd be home soon, based on what she'd read about the conference in the papers. Freed of worry about horses and her father, Carole had settled in to a pleasant visit with the Atwoods. She was always on time for dinner and she was as happy to help out at the Atwoods' as she was at home. Their house almost felt like home now, too.

Carole picked up her grooming bucket and went to work on Starlight. Next to her, her two best friends were doing the same for their horses. What a trio they were, happy as could be as long as they were together and as long as that "together" included horses.

Now, an even happier piece of news was that Lisa was back to within normal range on her schoolwork. She wasn't going to kill herself, literally or figuratively, about getting straight A-pluses. Straight As would be good enough for her. And Stevie? Well, Carole and Lisa never had figured out what her problem was. Ever since their trip through the woods, Stevie had been relaxed and cheerful—so cheerful that Carole suspected she was keeping a secret, but Carole didn't have a hint as to what it might be.

Secret-keeping wasn't Stevie's strong point. In fact, Lisa and Carole talked about it once, and the longest either of them could remember Stevie keeping a secret to herself was fourteen hours—and she'd slept for eight of them!

The only sour note these days was their sad memories of Delilah. After he had returned from the woods, Max had arranged to have her body picked up. The girls wanted to have Delilah buried on Pine Hollow property, but that was impossible because of the disease that had killed her. The last they saw of her was when a large van took her away. They had their memories, though, and those were precious indeed.

Carole tugged at a knot in Starlight's mane, only vaguely aware that someone else was walking up to them. The person stopped next to the three girls. It was Mrs. Johnson, the woman who had been taking lessons from Max.

"Stephanie?" Mrs. Johnson said.

Stevie looked up at her in surprise. "Uh, yeah?" she responded. That was Stevie's name all right, but not one she used much.

"I didn't know that was your real name," said Mrs. Johnson.

"I don't hear it much," Stevie said. "Unless my mother is really angry with me—or sometimes a new teacher will call me that on the first day of school."

"But you signed your letter that way," said Mrs. Johnson. "Well, I certainly know how that is. It's really no different from my situation."

Stevie was a little confused, but Mrs. Johnson had always seemed like a nice woman, so it would only be polite to wait and see what she wanted. Carole and Lisa listened, as rapt and as confused as Stevie.

"When I was born, my parents named me Elizabeth. It's a lovely name, just as Stephanie is a lovely name, but it's sort of a mouthful, if you know what I mean."

"Sure," Stevie said.

"Especially with my maiden name—Wallingford. It's just not fair to make somebody go through seven syllables to get one person's name. So my parents called me Betty, saving me two syllables every time I introduced myself!"

Stevie smiled. Then a bell started ringing. *Wallingford* sounded very familiar. But she couldn't place it yet.

"Of course, none of that mattered much when I married Mickey Johnson. That's a simple last name and can take a fancy first name, but by then I was so used to being called Betty that I stuck with it most of the time. Except when I started writing."

"Elizabeth Wallingford Johnson?" Stevie said incredulously.

"That's me," Mrs. Johnson said, offering her hand to shake.

Stevie shook it. "I had no idea," she said.

"Well, I could tell that," said Mrs. Johnson. "And there's no reason why you should. You know me as a rider, and that's the way I know you, too. You didn't know I was a writer as well, nor did I know that you were one of my readers—until I got your wonderful letter."

Stevie gulped. She'd expected an answer—but not in person! She had about fourteen questions she wanted to ask, but at the moment she was so stunned that she couldn't speak. It was a very unusual circumstance for Stevie Lake to be speechless!

"Anyway, I did love your letter. I was so excited that you'd found that rock. That rock was my whole inspiration for the book."

"It was Hallie's?" Stevie asked.

Mrs. Johnson shook her head. "No, it was mine. I've been walking and riding through these woods for years and I've always known that rock. The cave is so cozy—"

Lisa and Carole looked at one another. They'd been totally lost, but now they realized that they knew the rock, too, and they knew exactly what Stevie and Mrs. Johnson were talking about.

"—and that mark looks just like an arrow. Well, Stevie, it just suggested the whole story to me."

"But what about Hallie's diary?" Stevie asked. "Isn't that real?"

"Oh, sure," said Mrs. Johnson. "There is a diary by an escaped slave named Hallie, but it doesn't say anything about the rock. It's very sketchy, in fact. She only mentions in passing that she'd escaped to Canada on the Underground Railroad. Everything in the book, except

194

the name of the woman and the fact of her escape, was made up by me."

"Everything?"

"It's a novel, Stevie," Mrs. Johnson explained. "The whole thing is fiction, a made-up story."

"But it seemed so *real*," said Stevie. "Like I was there."

Mrs. Johnson smiled. "That's what I loved about your letter to me, when you said that. If I make a story feel real to you, then I've done my job."

"You did," said Stevie.

"Really well," Carole added.

"Absolutely," said Lisa.

"You girls read the book, too?" asked Mrs. Johnson.

"Well, Stevie kept talking about it," said Carole. "We just had to. Oh, and incidentally, if you get another letter suggesting that the rock is real and is in Willow Creek, Virginia, you don't have to answer it," she added shyly. "I mean, I think you've already answered it."

"Um, make that three," Lisa said. Carole and Stevie both looked at her, and then the three of them burst into laughter. Mrs. Johnson joined them.

"This feels like the beginning of a fan club!" said Mrs. Johnson. "I guess I'd better write another book now!"

"Please do!" Stevie said.

"And we promise to write you about it!" Lisa added. Mrs. Johnson thanked them all and then left the stable.

They were still laughing together when they finished

their grooming. Carole dropped her polishing rag into her bucket.

"This boy's going back to his stall for a snack, and then I think it's time for the three of us to go over to TD's for a treat. Anybody here want to have a Saddle Club meeting?"

"Last one there is a rotten egg!" Stevie declared.

The race was on.

## ABOUT THE AUTHOR

BONNIE BRYANT is the author of more than a hundred books about horses, including The Saddle Club series, The Saddle Club Super Editions, the Pony Tails series, and Pine Hollow, which follows the Saddle Club girls into their teens. She has also written novels and movie novelizations under her married name, B. B. Hiller.

Ms. Bryant began writing The Saddle Club in 1986. Although she had done some riding before that, she intensified her studies then and found herself learning right along with her characters Stevie, Carole, and Lisa. She claims that they are all much better riders than she is.

Ms. Bryant was born and raised in New York City. She still lives there, in Greenwich Village, with her two sons.